BEAUTIFULLY BACKED

CANDIED CRUSH #8

CHARITY PARKERSON

—Warning: This book is intended for readers over the age of 18.

Copyright © 2020 Charity Parkerson
Editor: BZ Hercules & Consultants
Photographer: Pick-Your-Pic
ISBN: 978-1-946099-78-5
All rights reserved.

INTRODUCTION

A single night of powerful connection collides with a cruel twist of fate. No matter the outcome, Sergio and Tobin are meant to be.

Sergio went from the streets to being one of the highest-paid soccer players in the world. For the most part, he has tried to stay humble. The change in his circumstances doesn't mean his life is easy now. He meets a lot of users and has a hard time saying no. Tobin is the first person he's met since hitting it big who doesn't want a thing from him. Yet Tobin needs him more than Sergio could possibly know.

Tobin has no clue Sergio is famous. In a moment

of living life to the fullest while he can, Tobin takes Sergio home for the night. While it is the greatest night of his life, he has no plans to repeat the experience. Everything recently changed for him and Tobin is in no place to start a relationship. He must accept Sergio as the temporary gift he is, except he doesn't take into account Sergio's determination.

Sergio isn't the type to be pushed aside. Tobin is in his sights now. Unlike everyone else, Tobin deserves Sergio's help and he's not taking no for an answer. All he can do now is hope that life doesn't steal Tobin before Sergio can save him.

ONE

CONSIDERING Sergio's friend Valor had made it to forty without ever being married, Sergio was more than a little surprised—in a good way—to be sitting at the guy's engagement party. It thrilled Sergio to no end to see Valor finally settling down. Although it was a little strange to see Valor marrying a man two years older than Sergio's twenty-four, but who was he to judge. When it came to love, Sergio wasn't exactly killing it. For someone with a five-million-dollar-a-year contract with an L.A. pro soccer team, the Lancers, and several lucrative contracts with advertising agencies, he would have thought he would have better luck with the guys, but no. He only met users or cheats... or both. That didn't mean

Sergio planned to quit. In fact, he couldn't stop gravitating toward Valor's man's best friend, Tobin.

Tobin was a tiny blond with light green eyes and a blush that made all the muscles in Sergio's stomach tighten with lust. The moment Sergio had walked into the engagement party, his gaze had found Tobin and his feet had been headed Tobin's way before Sergio could have a second thought. While Sergio would normally be a little guarded with someone new, he was a good ninety percent certain that Tobin had no idea who Sergio was—other than being Valor's friend, of course. Sergio couldn't stop flirting with him. Watching the man blush was too much fun.

"Tell me, Tobin, what's your favorite color? Do you want to sit on my lap?"

Tobin's gaze dropped to the floor. A gorgeous blush touched his cheeks. "It's red. What about you?"

"It's green. The exact shade of your eyes, to be more specific. You're a baker, right? What's your favorite food and do you plan to take me home tonight?"

Tobin met his stare again. "I'm a pastry chef and Mexican food, but not like Tex Mex. Do you know what I mean?" Tobin became more animated, talking with his hands. "Like, not the California style bastardized version of Mexican food, but like authentic. Does that make sense?"

A laugh burst from Sergio. "Yeah. I'm Hispanic."

Tobin blushed again as Sergio pointed out the obvious. "Oh, yeah. Sorry."

"Don't apologize. You're adorable." Sergio barely stopped himself from stroking Tobin's jawline. He looked like he had soft skin. Sergio wanted to find out. "I love pizza," Sergio added, hoping to soothe Tobin's embarrassment. "I'm not a chef, like you, but I sure as hell can cook you some authentic Mexican food. That's another reason you should take me home. I'd make it worth your while." Sergio eyed Tobin's body with every ounce of heat he felt. He bit his bottom lip. Damn. Tobin looked sexy in his gray button-down shirt and dark jeans. "In more ways than one," Sergio added, so there would be no misunderstandings about what would happen if Tobin took him home. He quickly changed tactics again, trying to keep Tobin off balance so he wouldn't run away. "Do you like watching sports?"

Tobin curled his nose. "Not especially. It's not that I hate them, or anything. I just get bored and stop paying attention. Since you asked, I'm assuming you do. Which is your favorite?"

"*Fútbol.*" Sergio stared intently at Tobin, looking for any signs that the man played games with him. Tobin wouldn't be the first man to pretend not to know him in hopes of getting closer.

Tobin's forehead furrowed. He looked adorably confused. "Do you mean American football or soccer?"

A smile exploded across Sergio's face. Tobin wasn't playing him. He really didn't know Sergio played professionally. "Soccer."

Tobin's expression cleared. He smiled. "Oh. My mom tried to make me play that when I was four. She said I refused to run back and forth with my team. Instead, I kept dropping to the ground and crawling around so I could pick dandelions."

Sergio couldn't stop smiling at the laughter in Tobin's eyes. "I bet you weren't much smaller than you are now."

To his surprise, Tobin's smile slipped away. "I'm sure."

Sergio hadn't meant to insult him. He found Tobin adorable. Apparently, he had hit an insecurity. Sergio hated that. He wasn't that guy. He liked making people smile. Sergio scrambled to expose a weakness too so they would be even. "I grew up in the streets, living in homeless camps and shelters. That's how I met Valor. He was one of the cops who spent time with the teens. We would play basketball and whatnot. He's been good to me—made sure I didn't stay without a home, you know? How did you become best friends with a famous actor like Reid?" Sergio had to keep Tobin from asking too much about his past. He still wasn't ready for Tobin to find out he was famous in certain circles. Sergio liked that Tobin thought he was just some guy.

Tobin was back to looking open again. His insecurities had disappeared. "I have a deal set up with the Coastal Arts Center where Reid does a lot of his theater work. A few days a week, I restock their green room with baked goods to keep the crew fed. Reid is a force of nature. He just kind of adopted me as his friend. I don't remember being consulted. It was like I was there working one minute, and Reid swept me out the door the next. He talked a mile a minute while taking us to lunch." A sexy smile touched Tobin's lips. "I don't think I even told him my name until we were leaving the restaurant. It's pretty much been like that ever since."

Even though Tobin laughed at the memory, Sergio didn't want Tobin to walk away with a similar story about him. "What's your last name?"

Tobin looked taken aback by the question, but he still immediately answered. "Sader. What's yours?"

"Costa. How old are you?"

"Twenty-four." Tobin kept immediately answering Sergio's questions without an ounce of reluctance.

Sergio's smile was out of control. "Me too. You never answered me about sitting on my lap."

Another blush exploded across Tobin's face. He dropped his gaze again.

Sergio shook his head. "Damn." Even Sergio heard the humor in his curse. "The shy ones get me every time."

To Sergio's surprise, Tobin's gaze lifted and met his with a bravery Sergio had never seen in his life. "I'm not shy."

A wicked smirk touched Sergio's lips. He couldn't stop it from happening. Tobin tempted him on every level. "Prove it."

Tobin stood. A surge of disappointment shot through Sergio. It seemed he had gone too far. When Sergio didn't move, Tobin held his hand out. "Are we going, or not?"

Sergio shot to his feet and linked fingers with Tobin. No way in hell would he turn down Tobin's offer.

Tobin didn't immediately head for the door. His gaze swept the room. "Reid picked me up, so you'll have to drive."

"Sounds good." Especially since Sergio had no intention of leaving his Porsche here. He couldn't tear his eyes away from Tobin. Sergio couldn't believe Tobin truly meant to take him home.

Tobin still seemed a bit absent. "I thought to tell Reid bye, but I don't see him."

Sergio nudged Tobin toward the door. "I saw Valor and Reid sneaking away a few minutes ago. I get the feeling they're not worrying about their guests right now." He forced his stare from Tobin and searched the room with his gaze. He spotted Dawson nearby. Dawson was like a son to Valor. Sergio knew he could trust Dawson to let Valor know they had gone. He caught Dawson's eye and signaled they were leaving. Dawson nodded, and Sergio steered Tobin toward the door. "Dawson will let Reid know I'm taking you home."

"Okay."

Tobin didn't sound like he had any doubts, but Sergio held tightly to his hand anyhow as they headed out. He had Tobin now. Sergio wouldn't lose his chance if he had anything to say about it. He knew a good thing when he saw one.

ALL OF THESE THOUGHTS ABOUT HOW HE couldn't believe he was doing this kept trying to shove their way inside Tobin's head. Tobin kept pushing them away. Sergio's gorgeous car said a lot about how far out of Tobin's league he was, but Tobin didn't care. This was for one night only. Sergio had been on his bucket list since they met at Valor's place months earlier. Tobin wouldn't let any amount of good sense get in the way this one time. He only had this one life. Tobin intended to live it his way.

As they pulled into the parking lot of Road Clan bar, Tobin worried Sergio might take one look at where he lived and realize how far beneath him Tobin was. But if he ran, then Tobin would know Sergio wasn't worth his time anyhow. So he squared his shoulders and directed Sergio to the back-parking lot of the biker bar.

"Circle the building. There are a couple of reserved parking spots back there."

"Okay." Sergio dragged out the word, as if confused by the directions Tobin gave. He still followed Tobin's instructions without argument.

Tobin pointed at an empty space next to his delivery van. "You can park there."

Without a word, Sergio swung wide and backed into the spot. As they slid from the car, Sergio's alarm chirped.

Tobin flashed him a smile. "Don't worry. You're my guest. Your car is safer here than anywhere in the world. No one would mess with the guys in this place."

Sergio shrugged. "I'm not worried."

Tobin waited for Sergio so he could take his hand. When their fingers linked, he headed for a metal staircase next to the building. He spotted Damon through the bar's window as they headed up. He gave the burly bar owner a small wave. Damon returned to gesture.

"You live above a biker bar? Isn't that noisy as hell?"

Like the move had been choreographed to coincide with Sergio's question, the loud music blaring from inside lowered. Tobin chuckled. "No. The guys know I live upstairs and Damon, the owner, he makes sure they keep it down when I'm home. Everyone who comes here are regulars and it's like a big family." Tobin didn't add that he didn't know what he would do without these guys. Some days were much harder than others, and these burly bikers with hearts of gold kept him going.

As they came through the door, Sergio looked around. Tobin knew what he saw. His apartment was pretty small but cozy. The brown overstuffed couch had been chosen for comfort rather than style. He owned a smallish TV and had more books than most. His kitchen was nicer than the rest of the apartment, but that was because he worked from home. Thankfully, Damon let him use his storeroom for most of his supplies. Otherwise, Tobin wouldn't have anywhere to sit. From nowhere, Tobin's nerves frayed. He had invited a stranger to his place. Sergio was obviously rich and incredibly sexy. He could have anyone. Tobin's apartment had to be the worst place Sergio had ever stepped foot in since he left the streets. What had he been thinking bringing Sergio home? Then Sergio's gaze moved his way and didn't budge. The dark scruff on his jaw made Tobin's palms itch to touch it. His dark green eyes sparkled with intelligence. Tobin wanted to hear his every thought. This was only for one night. Tobin had to keep reminding himself of that fact.

A sweet-looking smile touched Sergio's lips. "It's okay if you've changed your mind. I'm cool to just hang out and talk or whatever."

Something about Sergio always seeing his shyness and discomfort too clearly made Tobin want to be the opposite. Sergio was completely out of Tobin's league. Tobin wanted to be on his level. There was only one way Tobin could achieve that. He had to be braver than he felt.

"You should strip." Honest to god, no one was more surprised than him by the demand. He wasn't this person, but Tobin didn't take it back. It was too late now. He had already been way too bold, and now he wanted to see where this insanity took him.

Sergio shrugged off the open button-down shirt he wore over a skintight slick-looking t-shirt. Tobin held his breath as Sergio tossed the shirt aside and untucked the shirt from his black pants. With the shirt untucked, Sergio reached over his head and pulled the material over his head and off his body in one smooth motion. Tobin moved a step closer. He couldn't stop himself. Sergio was every bit as sleek beneath his shirt as Tobin expected. Sergio had a runner's body. Each muscle was well defined. Not like a guy who spent too much time at the gym, but like a man who used his body like a tool. Sergio looked as if he had been carved from marble. Tobin's hand reached out with no permission from his brain. His skin looked pale against the dark skin of Sergio's torso as he traced the lines of Sergio's sculpted abs.

"Jesus. What's it like to be flawless?" Tobin

couldn't stop the question. He had always wondered what it felt like to be beautiful like Sergio.

"I wouldn't know since I have a thousand imperfections."

Tobin wanted to roll his eyes at that obvious lie, but he was too busy enjoying the sensation of Sergio's soft skin beneath his fingertips. Hunger rose inside Tobin, stamping out all hints of discomfort. Tobin went to work on Sergio's belt. The leather felt expensive as Tobin pulled it loose. "I want to see the rest." Tobin no longer recognized himself. He wasn't the type of guy who stripped men bare and demanded to see their bodies. Sergio made him feel a level of desire he had never experienced before. It was like Tobin starved for him.

Tobin easily sent Sergio's pants and boxer briefs to the floor. He stooped to strip them all the way off along with Sergio's shoes. When he glanced up and found himself staring at Sergio's cock, Tobin disappeared inside himself. There was no fear or embarrassment. Tobin could do anything without regret. He was in control here. After all, he was still fully dressed. Sergio was the one on display. Tobin had all the power. So he licked Sergio's dick.

Sergio hissed.

The feeling of control grew in Tobin's chest,

making him bolder by the second. He wrapped his fingers around Sergio's cock and sucked the tip.

"*De puta madre*," Sergio whispered as he buried his fingers in Tobin's hair and held on.

Tobin put his heart into pleasuring Sergio. He didn't think. Tobin simply acted, following the sounds Sergio made to keep up whatever actions made him the loudest. He felt Sergio's muscles tense and Tobin braced himself for Sergio to blow. Instead, he found himself on his feet. Sergio's mouth covered his. It wasn't until their tongues brushed that Tobin realized he had sucked Sergio's dick before they even had their first kiss. It was like he didn't recognize himself anymore. A small part of him was horrified by his actions. The rest of him was mesmerized by Sergio's kiss. His kiss was a mixture of teasing and hot. He made Tobin chase him, then rewarded him by sucking hard on Tobin's bottom lip. Tobin scratched at Sergio's chest, trying to get closer.

"Where's your bedroom?"

Tobin motioned down the hall. "The only open door."

"Let's go." Sergio shuffled Tobin that way, walking him backward while still trying to steal his kisses.

Sergio kept an eye out, steering Tobin around

furniture until they reached the bed. At the edge, he began stripping Tobin. "Tell me you have condoms here and I don't have to go out to my car."

Tobin nodded as he helped Sergio get him out of his clothes. "In the top drawer of the nightstand. There's a box."

Sergio looked between Tobin and the table and back again, as if he couldn't decide what to do first.

Tobin took charge again. "Get on the bed."

At Tobin's drill sergeant tone, Sergio didn't hesitate. He scrambled onto the bed and settled onto his back, hard and waiting. Tobin quickly finished undressing before gathering the lube and a condom. He tore into the package before joining Sergio. As he straddled Sergio's thighs, the feeling of being powerful overtook him again.

Tobin rolled the condom down Sergio's length. He had a nice cock. Long and not too wide. Tobin wanted it. "I'm sure you probably hear this all the time, but you're gorgeous. Stunning, actually." Tobin kept talking as he lubed the outside of the condom. "Sometimes, it's hard for me to look at you directly— like staring into the sun, I guess. You're too hot for someone who gets burned as easily as I do." He knew he was being fanciful and probably didn't make sense to Sergio. Tobin didn't care. He wouldn't see

Sergio again after tonight. Tobin wanted Sergio to understand—at least partially—why. Sergio could easily break Tobin's heart, and that wasn't something he could handle right now. Tobin stared down at the oily mess he had made. His mouth watered. "Damn. I kind of wish I held off on the lube. I want to suck your dick again."

"Fuck. You could make me blow just by talking. I can't take it." Sergio rolled, tucking Tobin beneath him and pinning him to the bed. His tongue invaded Tobin's mouth and sparred with Tobin's tongue. Tobin's dick throbbed, needing attention. He wanted to rub against Sergio like a cat and hump him. Sergio rocked. The move massaged Tobin's cock, pulling a gasp from him.

Tobin ripped his mouth away and bit Sergio's shoulder. "Stop playing and fuck me."

At his demand, Sergio hooked Tobin's leg with his arm, pulling it higher. His blunt head pushed against the tight muscles surrounding Tobin's asshole. Tobin bit Sergio again and Sergio surged upward, impaling him. A cry tore from Tobin's throat. He went wild, shoving and clawing until he had Sergio on his back again. Once he had Sergio where he wanted him, Tobin braced one hand on Sergio's chest and rode him like a fucking horse while jacking off. Tobin was too horny to be embarrassed. He needed release. Sergio's sexy body had been teasing him all night. Tobin wanted to shoot cum all over it—like marking his territory.

Tobin leaned back, using the strength in his thighs to keep up the pace while using Sergio's dick the way he liked. His eyes fell closed as he lost himself in the pleasure of Sergio's cock, the sensation of his palm, and the sounds Sergio made. He was a prisoner of pleasure. The world and all its problems had disappeared the moment Tobin sat on Sergio's dick. He wanted to ride it all night, but pressure beat at his crown, pulsing and wanting to be set free. Tobin stroked faster and thrust harder, taking what he wanted. The world balanced on the edge of a knife for half a heartbeat. Then ecstasy shook Tobin's soul. He cried out as his body convulsed. Tobin stroked out every drop of cum. Sergio flipped him onto his back and slammed inside, making tiny aftershocks ripple through him. All Tobin could do was gasp for air as Sergio shouted his pleasure and shook in his arms. Tobin held on tighter as Sergio fought for air against his ear.

"Holy shit. Wow. Damn."

A smile stretched Tobin's lips over Sergio's reaction.

"What are you doing for the rest of your life?"

A chuckle burst from Tobin at Sergio's question. "I don't know."

"I do," Sergio said, rolling onto his back and tucking Tobin against him to snuggle. "I need more of that. That was... wow."

It had been earth-shattering. Tobin didn't know where all that bravery and take-charge attitude had come from, but it had been amazing. He wouldn't forget this night Sergio had given him. It would have to last him for the remainder of what could be a very short life. Tobin didn't know if he felt better or worse now. Dying wasn't for the weak.

A BEEPING NOISE SOUNDED IN THE DISTANCE, pulling Sergio from the sleep of the dead. He blinked at his surroundings. It was too dark to make out much, but nothing looked familiar. The beeping continued as the memories washed over him. A smile slowly stretched his lips. It fell when he realized he was alone. His gaze shot around the room. A clock with huge red numbers sat on top of the nightstand, proclaiming it to be three thirty. Sergio assumed it meant a.m. since it was dark as shit outside. All his clothes were still in the living room. With a shrug, Sergio rolled from the bed and followed the sound of the alarm.

He found Tobin in the kitchen shushing the timer on the oven and trying to get it to stop. The scent of fresh-baked pastry filled the air. Sergio leaned his elbows on the bar that separated the living room from the kitchen and watched Tobin fight to stop the noise. Two pans of croissants already sat cooling on the counter while Tobin pulled more from the oven. Tobin turned and startled, nearly dropping the hot pans as he spotted Sergio watching him.

He blushed. "Sorry. I've never realized how loud these timers are or how long they go on until I was trying not to wake you."

Sergio shrugged. "No worries. Sleep is overrated. This view is much better than anything I've ever dreamed about." Tobin went back to looking shy, fascinating Sergio. He didn't for one second think it was an act, but he loved the way Tobin tossed it aside the moment he got aroused. Still, he liked Tobin and wanted him to be comfortable around him all the time. Sergio tried toning his flirtatious nature down. "So this is what you do, huh? You wake up in the middle of the night and make rolls."

"They're croissants," Tobin said with a laugh.

"And yes, this is what I do. Would you like to try one?"

There was no way Sergio could say no to Tobin's hopeful expression. Plus, they smelled delicious. "Yeah. Why do you think I'm standing here in the buff? The promise of food pulled me from my sleep."

Tobin shook his head, but his smile never wavered. He grabbed a napkin and set a fresh roll on top before sliding it Sergio's way. "Don't eat it yet," he fussed before quickly turning away. Sergio's gaze ate Tobin alive as he turned away and dug something from the refrigerator. He wore a long T-shirt and short workout shorts. His blond curls were a mess and Sergio couldn't look away. Tobin headed back Sergio's way and set a small open container and butter knife by the roll. "Try a bite with and without the strawberry preserves."

Sergio nodded, since this seemed to be important to Tobin. Before he could take a bite, Tobin held up his hands. "Wait!"

Sergio blinked. "What?"

"You don't have any food allergies, do you?"

With a snort, Sergio took a bite. The flakes melted in his mouth. Honey and butter seemed to explode across his taste buds. "*Dios mío.*" It was amazing. Sergio scooped some of the strawberry preserves onto the next bite and found himself in heaven as he chewed. "Holy shit. You should marry me right now. Like, what would it take to get you to say yes?"

Tobin snorted, but he didn't stop smiling. "Would you like some coffee or something to go with it? You're welcome to as much as you want. I always make extra in case any of my customers need a bigger order when I get there."

"Coffee sounds good. Do you need some help?"

Tobin shook his head and turned away. Sergio went in search of his boxer briefs before claiming a stool at the bar. He enjoyed watching Tobin move around the kitchen, boxing up pastries. It was homey —like a normal life. Sergio had gone from the streets to being a millionaire seemingly overnight. He hadn't really gotten to experience this kind of life since his mom had passed away. It felt good in his chest. As he stared at Tobin, the emotions stirring inside of him had him noticing other things about Tobin—like the fact that Tobin moved slow, as if in pain. There were dark marks under both his eyes, making him look like he had lost a fight.

"I think I kept you up too late. If I had known you get up this early, I might have made you go to bed earlier."

Tobin flashed him a tight smile as he poured Sergio a cup of coffee. "Don't worry. After I finish all my deliveries today, I can come home and sleep all day. It evens out. Sugar or cream?"

Sergio nodded. "Please."

Tobin passed him the cup before passing along a sugar shaker and creamer container. He kept up the conversation while Sergio doctored his coffee. "I'm still sorry I woke you up. I didn't know if you needed to be up by a certain time, but I didn't figure you had to be up as early as me."

Sergio tossed a quick glance around the room. It was creeping closer to four. He had practice this morning, but not until eight. "What time do you have to start your deliveries?"

"In about an hour," Tobin answered as he went back to boxing up the rolls. "I pretty much have my route down to a science, so it doesn't take as long. Damon comes in to accept beer and liquor deliveries around ten. I usually make it back by then and deliver to him last. Full circle," he said, talking with his hands. "Of course, I don't charge him. We have a deal worked out where I use part of his storeroom space and he gets baked goods for free. I'm pretty lucky to have this place."

Sergio worked on downing another roll. He

spoke around his bite. "If you ask me, he's the lucky one. That marriage offer is still on the table."

Tobin chuckled. It was a soft and sexy sound. "You strike me as a popular guy. I don't like to share, so it's probably best I decline."

Even though he had been joking about marriage, Sergio was oddly disappointed. He liked Tobin. Sergio found himself confessing things he had never said aloud. "I'm not popular among people who actually know me." He chose his words carefully, picking through each one while trying not to reveal too much about himself. Sergio liked that Tobin didn't know him. "The people I spend the most time with don't like me very much. They think I'm too cocky and conceited. So I think they work extra hard to take me down a peg, but the harder they work at it, the faker and more obnoxious I get. That probably doesn't make a lot of sense."

Tobin held a coffee mug between his hands and stared at Sergio in silence while listening to every word Sergio said. After a moment, he shrugged. "Fuck 'em."

A laugh burst from Sergio. He didn't know why, but Tobin's words shocked him as much as amused him. Sergio had expected Tobin to have some magic advice because he seemed so much more adult-like than Sergio felt. Sergio didn't feel equipped to handle as much as he had on his plate most of the time. Mostly, he just felt like a tired joke.

Tobin didn't laugh. He set his cup aside and circled the bar. Sergio turned in his seat. Tobin held Sergio's stare as he moved to stand between Sergio's knees. His hands ran up Sergio's thighs, but his gaze never wavered from holding Sergio's. "I'm one hundred percent serious, so listen to me. Life is short." Sergio couldn't explain it, but he hung on every word. Tobin looked like he had all the answers as he held Sergio's stare. "It's way too brief to care about other people's opinions. Don't fake at being insufferable if someone doesn't like you for you. Be obnoxious for real. Fuck their feelings. At the end of the day, you're the only person who has to live with your thoughts and feelings, so live your life and be happy. I promise you they're not thinking about you when you're not around, so don't give them your headspace either." Tobin's mouth lifted in one corner. "If it helps or matters at all, I like you— cockiness and all—and I don't like many people."

Sergio found himself tracing the line of Tobin's jaw. A thousand thoughts crowded his head. He had never met anyone like Tobin. Tobin was beautiful and passionate. He was obviously used to grinding it out every day for his money. Tobin wasn't like the men who usually chased Sergio. He made Sergio want to be the one doing all the work.

The timer started beeping again, pulling Tobin's attention away from Sergio. As much as Sergio wanted to keep Tobin right where he was, he couldn't ruin Tobin's hard work. Sergio let Tobin rush away. He went back to drinking his coffee and watching Tobin move around the kitchen. Sergio would keep seeing Tobin. He had his own hustling to do today, but this wasn't over. They were starting something here. Sergio looked forward to seeing where things went. They had time, and Tobin definitely had his attention.

TWO

AFTER GETTING up at three a.m. to bake, finishing his deliveries for the day, and visiting his doctor, Tobin was beyond exhausted. He was at a point where it literally hurt to hold his eyes open. His body felt heavy—like he dragged himself through wet concrete. He was on his way to bed when the knock landed on his front door. Tobin moved to the window to look out. He peeked through the sheers and spotted Sergio at the door. Tobin's heart skipped a beat. It had been over a week since their night together. He looked really sexy today and he held a bouquet. As Tobin looked on, Sergio swiped his hand over his hair, as if checking to make sure it didn't stand on end. Tobin bit his bottom lip, trying not to smile. Sergio knocked again. Tobin wanted to answer, but he looked like hell and Sergio was supposed to be a one-night thing. He didn't understand why Sergio was back.

As Tobin looked on, Sergio checked his surroundings, as if trying to gauge if Tobin was home. He spent a second staring at Tobin's delivery van before leaning over the railing and looking inside the bar. Sergio quickly jogged down the steps and circled the building.

Tossing exhaustion to the wind, Tobin raced to the back stairs inside his apartment that led to the bar's storeroom. After sneaking down the steps, he tiptoed to the swinging door that separated the storeroom from the area behind the bar. Tobin bent at the waist and pushed the door open a hair as he spotted Sergio coming through the front door.

Sergio tossed a glance around the room, as if checking out the place before zeroing in on Damon behind the bar. Unfortunately, Damon spotted Tobin as Sergio reached the bar. Tobin pressed a finger to his lips and Damon quickly turned away.

"What can I get you?"

Sergio smiled.

Tobin's heart melted. Why did he have to be so damn sexy?

"Actually, I'm looking for the guy who lives upstairs, Tobin."

Damon shifted slightly, as if trying to keep Sergio's focus away from where Tobin hid. "What do you need with Tobin?"

Sergio made a nervous gesture with the flowers he held. "We're friends."

Tobin bit his bottom lip, trying to squelch a smile. They were friends. That much Tobin believed.

"Oh." Damon couldn't have sounded more confused. "I don't think he's home. He's likely still making his deliveries for the day. If you want, I can tell him you stopped by."

For a moment, Sergio seemed to think it over before shaking his head. "It's cool. I'll come back later." He perked up for a second, turning into the too smooth guy who had caught Tobin's attention from the first moment they met. Sergio held his hand out. "I'm Sergio, by the way." Goddamn. He said the words like Damon would be seeing a lot of him.

Damon shook his hand. "Damon."

Sergio nodded. "I figured. Tobin told me about you. He's says you're like family."

Oh, he was good, buttering up Damon. Very slick.

With a final knock on the countertop and goodbye, Sergio headed for the door. Tobin couldn't resist watching Sergio walk away. He always dressed with style and today was no different. In a thin button-down shirt left unbuttoned over a tight t-shirt, and jeans that sagged just enough to make Tobin want to slide them the rest of the way down, Tobin's mouth watered. He knew what that sleek body could do. Tobin would never forget.

Before he could regain his senses and scurry away, Damon pushed the door open. He tossed his hand towel over his shoulder and crossed his arms over his wide chest. His blue eyes flashed with laughter. A kind smile touched his lips as he stared at Tobin in his hiding spot. "Do you want to tell me what's going on?"

Tobin shrugged, feeling exposed. The huge ginger always hovered over Tobin, but Damon seemed twice as imposing today while Tobin tried keeping his secrets. Then Tobin's big mouth betrayed him. "You just met the guy I like way too much."

Damon's chest expanded on a deep breath. "So, naturally, that means you're hiding from him."

With his bottom lip between his teeth, Tobin

chewed while staring up at Damon. He didn't know how to respond.

For a moment, Damon stared at him in silence. His gaze moved over Tobin's features. Tobin knew what he saw. Both his eyes were black, and he had already lost weight. His skin was so pale now, it was almost translucent. Tobin was beyond exhausted. His legs felt like lead weights. With a shake of his head, Damon grabbed his towel and tossed it toward the bar.

"Come on, darling. You're supposed to be resting."

Tobin didn't have the strength to argue as Damon swept him from his feet and headed up the stairs.

"Jesus, baby. You're light as a feather. I'll fix you something to eat."

Tobin fought the urge to argue that Damon was too damn big. He had giant muscles and two feet too many in the height department. It was no damn wonder Tobin felt like a lightweight to him. Instead, he accepted that Damon tried to help. "Don't bother. Food won't stay down." There was no sense in sugarcoating things with Damon since he was the one who would likely be burying Tobin soon.

Damon didn't argue as he tucked Tobin into bed. "How much does that boy know?"

Tobin bit back a smile at Damon calling Sergio a boy. "He's the same age as me."

"You're a boy too," Damon said with a smile. "But judging by your avoidance, he knows nothing."

Tobin snuggled deeper beneath the covers, trying to fight the cold that settled into his bones. "Let me have this one thing, okay? It's nice having one person on the planet who doesn't pity me. He gave me one night of happy normalcy. I won't repay his kindness by letting him into my life. Hell, I'd make you get out if I could."

Damon snorted. "I'm sure. Too bad for you, I like staying where I'm not wanted."

Even though Tobin knew Damon was joking, he felt too bad to be anything less than serious. He might not have much longer. Tobin couldn't live with there being any chance Damon really believed that. "You're wanted." Even Tobin heard the sudden panic in his voice.

Damon sat at Tobin's hip so fast, it was like the man's knees gave out. He brushed his finger down Tobin's nose, as if trying to comfort him. "I know." He took an audible breath. "Do I need to call your mom?"

Tobin shook his head. "I don't want her missing work just to watch me sleep. I'm fine." They both knew it was a lie, but Tobin fully intended to pass out the second he was alone. Tobin's phone vibrated on the nightstand.

Damon grabbed the device and passed it Tobin's way. "Here. Call me if you need anything. I'm right downstairs. You know you're not putting me out. Okay?"

Tobin nodded.

Damon kissed his forehead and left Tobin alone with his phone. Tobin glanced at the face. He had a text from an unfamiliar number. As Tobin unlocked the device, a smile stretched his lips.

310-555-0987: *This is Sergio. I snagged your number from Valor. I stopped by your place, but you weren't home. Damon said you were probably out making deliveries, so sorry if I'm bugging you at work. Anyway, I hope I'm not making a huge fool of myself, but I'd like to see you again. If you just wanted one night of fun, that's cool.*

Even though Tobin knew it was a mistake, he saved Sergio's number to his phone. He likely wouldn't use it, but it was nice knowing he hadn't only been a one-night stand. The phone buzzed in his hand again before he could set it aside.

Sergio: *On second thought, it's not cool. I really like you. I haven't really liked anyone nice in a long time. So, I hope you text me back. I'd love to take you on a real date.*

A smile stretched Tobin's lips. Some of the heaviness in his chest lifted as he rolled to his side and cuddled with his phone. Sergio wanted to take him on a proper date. Tobin's eyes fell closed with that happy thought in his head. His breaths deepened. He liked Sergio too. A little too much. It was nice to be liked back. He let that dream carry him away until sleep claimed him and there was nothing anymore.

SERGIO STARED AT HIS PHONE, HOPING TOBIN returned his text before he left. He knew he should leave, but he also kind of hoped Tobin would come home while he waited. Sergio didn't know what kind of car Tobin drove. The only cars in the private lot behind the bar were the same ones that had been there the other night. An old work van, a Harley, and now Sergio's Porsche. Sergio stared so hard at his phone that his vision blurred. A knock on his window startled Sergio's heart into his throat.

He tried to play off the way he had jumped as he rolled down his window. The guy from the bar, Damon, stood patiently waiting for Sergio's attention. Sergio felt the need to explain why he was still sitting there like a stalker in the guy's parking lot.

"Sorry, man. I'll be gone in a second, but I don't text and drive."

Even though Damon smiled, Sergio got the impression that Damon had his number and knew exactly why he hadn't budged. "Don't apologize. I'm glad you're still here. I have a question."

Sergio was confused, but he was sitting in the dude's parking lot like a creeper, so he rolled with it. "All right."

Damon hesitated, as if having second thoughts. Then he jumped right in. "What are your intentions with Tobin?"

As much as Sergio wanted to point out that Damon wasn't Tobin's dad... at least, he didn't think Damon was Tobin's dad, Sergio was kind of glad someone was looking out for Tobin. "I intend to be part of his life." Sergio didn't have to think about it. He had always been the type to know what he wanted, and he always went hard at pursuing his dreams. Tobin seemed like a good guy and Sergio needed to see what was there with them.

Damon gave him a sharp nod. "Then you should know, he has cancer."

It was like getting punched in the chest. All Sergio could do was stare at Damon as Damon went down on one knee beside his car so he wouldn't have to stay bent at the waist. He held Sergio's stare and let him have it.

"This is the second time and it's hitting him much harder than last time. He's tired and doesn't want anyone suffering along with him. If not for Reid shoving his way into his life, and me being right here all the time, he wouldn't let anyone do anything for him. You need to really think about if this is what you want, because this is no joke. Tobin doesn't need a player in his life right now. He needs steady people who aren't afraid to fight for him because he's exhausted. I don't know if he'll make it."

Sergio had nothing. He hadn't expected this. There was a small part of him that screamed for him to drive away now. Cancer was some heavy shit. After all, he had watched his mom die from it. Then again, he had watched his mom fight and he had fought with her, so he wasn't blindly falling into a mess he didn't understand. He knew his opponent and he wasn't the type to back down. If nothing else, Tobin felt like a friend. He had stood still and listened to Sergio complain about his problems, even though they barely knew each other. Tobin wasn't like everyone else in Sergio's life, and Sergio wasn't a bitch. He didn't ditch his friends when times were tough.

"What kind of cancer?"

Damon's light blue gaze never wavered from Sergio. "Leukemia. He's just started treatment this week, so it's really kicking his ass."

Sergio nodded. He thought about how tired Tobin had looked when Sergio left him the other day. "What can I do to help?"

A hint of a smile touched Damon's lips. "Don't toy with his feelings. Either be here or don't come back. Like I said, you should take some time to think about it."

This dude didn't know Sergio. "Okay. I've thought about it. What can I do to help?"

Damon's smile turned blinding. His eyes crinkled in the corners. He shook his head. "Come on. I'll let you in. He's probably asleep by now."

"You mean he's here?" Sergio didn't mean to sound so offended, but Tobin hadn't answered the door and Damon had told him Tobin wasn't home.

Damon nodded. "Word of warning, though, he

won't make it easy for you to invade his life. He's pretty determined to go this alone."

Sergio rolled up his window and stepped from the car. "Yeah, well, I'm pretty much a pain in everyone's ass. He'll get used to me refusing to budge." He dipped back inside when he realized he forgot Tobin's flowers. When he straightened, Sergio found Damon eyeing him strangely with his hardened stare—like the man had seen too many bad things. Sergio felt exposed. "What?"

Damon shook his head. "Just surprised, I guess. You seem to have a lot of substance for a professional athlete. Other than Reid, most of the famous people who find their way here are shallow assholes."

"I wasn't aware you knew me." Another thought hit before he got too offended. "Do you have a lot of famous people finding their way here?"

Damon shrugged. "You'd be surprised."

Before he could stop it, a snort escaped Sergio. "It's weird when people call me famous. I don't really think of myself that way, and Tobin one hundred percent has no idea who I am."

Damon laughed. "Oh, yeah. He wouldn't. Tobin *hates* watching sports. If I have it on in the bar, he'll go upstairs—like that's his cue to find something else to do." Damon led Sergio inside through the bar and behind the counter through a door that hid a different stairway. He motioned toward the door at the top. "It's unlocked. Like I said, he's probably asleep."

Sergio gave Damon a sharp nod and tried to make sure his hair wasn't standing on end—like it had a tendency to do. "Thanks, man. I'll find a way to repay you."

Damon shook his head. "Nope. Just treat my boy good so I don't have to break your legs and end your career and we'll be even."

Even though Damon smiled through the entire threat, he didn't doubt Damon meant every word. Sergio dipped his chin and accepted the warning before heading up the stairs. He got threatened all the time. That came with getting paid to compete. People took their sports pretty damn seriously. In this case, though, Damon's words were no threat. Sergio wasn't weak.

The apartment was completely silent as Sergio came through the door. Sergio headed straight for the bedroom. There was a lump in Tobin's bed. Sergio moved to that side of the bed and set Tobin's roses on the nightstand. He toed off his shoes and peeled off his overshirt. After tossing the button down aside, Sergio climbed into bed next to Tobin. Tobin immediately rolled into his arms and snuggled his face against the crook of Sergio's neck.

"Thank you for the flowers. Is it wrong that I find it sexy that you've taken up breaking and entering for me?" He sounded so weak and tired that Sergio's heart twisted in his chest.

Sergio chuckled as he pressed his lips to Tobin's temple. "What can I say? I'll go pretty far when I want something."

Tobin took an audible breath. "You always smell good."

"Go back to sleep, *mi alma*. I just came to hold you."

Judging by Tobin's steady breathing, he didn't need to be told. Sergio wasn't the least bit tired, but he settled in for the long haul. While he understood Damon's need to threaten him, no one really knew him. Sergio knew what it was like to suffer alone. He was a survivor. The things he had done to stay alive would shock people if they knew. Good people deserved good things, but life seemed to only give the best people nothing but shit. Sergio was only one person and he couldn't make a huge difference in the world, but he could do this. He had met a nice guy and he wasn't walking away. Lots of people had given up on him over the years, but he owed it to the

38

ones who hadn't to be a good man. He would be here when Tobin woke up. He would help however he could, and maybe—just maybe—Sergio would hate his life a little less afterward. Sergio believed. After all, he already felt a million times better while just holding Tobin. They had been meant to meet. For once, Sergio had no doubts.

THREE

SERGIO HAD FANTASTIC LIPS. Tobin spent much longer than necessary staring at them. When Sergio had climbed into bed with him, Tobin had been so out of his head with exhaustion that he hadn't known if Sergio was real. Now, here he was, sleeping peacefully at Tobin's side.

Tobin wanted to kiss him and bite a path down his body until Sergio cried his name. Sergio looked too peaceful to be disturbed. To save himself from temptation and to keep from overthinking things, Tobin slipped from the bed. He eyed the gorgeous roses on the nightstand. Why did Sergio have to be so nice? Damn it. Tobin wanted to kick him out, but not really. He was confused as hell. His good sense warred with his heart. The type of man who brought roses after what anyone else would have accepted as a one-night stand wasn't someone Tobin could just kick out. Fuck. He needed to make them even.

After a trip to the bathroom, Tobin slipped from the room, trying to be as quiet as possible. It was close to seven and the small market next door closed at eight. Tobin didn't have time to make himself presentable. He grabbed his shoes and headed out. Tobin needed to be quick. He didn't want Sergio to wake up alone and think he had been abandoned. That wasn't the path to making them even so he could shut Sergio from his life guilt free. Tobin would grab a few steaks and cook the guy a nice dinner. Then it would be adios with no hard feelings. Shit. Why did Sergio have to be fucking perfect?

Inside the small family-owned market next door, Tobin smiled at the older woman who worked most nights. He grabbed a hand basket and started making an internal list. Since Sergio could be vegan for all Tobin knew, he would grab some veggies too. Potatoes, for sure. Everyone liked those, right? He cut through the cereal aisle to get to the meat section faster. An orange box caught his eye as he passed. Tobin barely focused on it as he walked by. Then his feet froze to the floor. No. Tobin took two steps back. His gaze locked on to the box and didn't budge. It couldn't be. He grabbed the package from the shelf and stared harder at the image. In a red and black uniform, Sergio held a soccer ball between his hands, looking fierce. Tobin gaze slid to the signature in the corner. Sergio Costa. The room went hazy, making Tobin realize he had been holding his breath. He sucked air. Holy fucking shit. There was a guy, so famous that he was on a goddamn cereal box, in Tobin's bed. Tobin put the box back on the shelf. There was no way. Seriously, there was no goddamn way. There had to be two Sergios with the same last name and who looked exactly alike.

Tobin shopped while trapped in a haze. He fought the urge to go back down the cereal aisle and check again. Surely he hadn't seen correctly. Tobin tried to reason with himself. After all, he knew other famous people. Reid was a movie star. There was that one model who came into the bar sometimes. He was pretty sure there were a couple of guys who worked in porn that frequented that one coffee shop he went to occasionally. Tobin hadn't fucked any of those people. Jesus Christ. What was happening? No famous soccer player could possibly want him.

Tobin was as average as could be. He wasn't buff or even cut. Tobin was just... Tobin. He was a regular guy. He was short as hell, for fuck's sake. Tobin had to use a step stool to reach his salt in the upper cabinets. His hair was always a mess and he had a fairly nice ass, but that was it. This couldn't be happening.

After making the barest minimum of small talk with the cashier, Tobin carried his groceries home in a fog of confusion. Sergio's car still sat parked in the lot. The apartment was still silent as he came through the door. Tobin set everything he had bought for dinner on the counter while trapped in his thoughts. It was possible he deserved this shock. Tobin purposely hadn't asked any actual questions about Sergio's life. He hadn't wanted to know. If Tobin asked about Sergio's life, then that would make them more than a good time. More than a good time meant strings. Strings meant Sergio was part of Tobin's fucked-up life. Goddamn it. It was too late. He had seen that stupid box. Tobin bent at the waist and set his forehead on his crossed arms on top of the counter. He stared at the kitchen floor as he sucked air and tried clearing his mind.

A second shadow stretched across the floor.

Sergio's hands settled on Tobin's waist. He urged Tobin up and back until Tobin found himself wrapped in Sergio's embrace. Tobin's back fit perfectly against Sergio's chest—like they snapped together to make one piece. Sergio's lips brushed the shell of Tobin's ear. Goosebumps rose on Tobin's skin. Sergio moved from Tobin's ear to his neck, kissing a path to his shoulder. Tobin's body stirred to life.

"I just saw you on a cereal box."

Sergio froze with his lips pressed to Tobin's shoulder. He set his chin on Tobin's shoulder. "Is that why you were bent over in here, looking like you were having a panic attack? Are you freaking out about me, or are you still tired from starting your cancer treatment?"

Touché. "A little of both, I suppose."

"Okay. Come on, gorgeous. You're going back to bed and I'm cooking."

Tobin didn't budge. "You don't want this."

Sergio snorted. "What? I love steak. I'm an awesome cook too. You'll see."

"You know that's not what I meant." Tobin refused to back down. This was too important. "You're young, and—no doubt—active as hell. I'm sure you have a ton of friends and like to do a fuck ton of things I can't do right now. You don't want to be trapped with this. Please take the free pass I'm giving you and go live your life. I'm okay with knowing I had you for one night. Please don't do this to yourself."

To his surprise, Sergio held him tighter. Tobin's eyes filled with tears as Sergio pressed his face against Tobin's neck and kissed him. "I'm not okay with being a one-night stand."

"You're an idiot." The words came out in a choked whisper. He didn't understand why Sergio would choose to stay.

"So I've been told, but I'm also your friend. What would you do if the shoe was on the other foot?"

Tobin wanted to say he would run as fast as could in the opposite direction just so Sergio would leave, but he couldn't. Tobin had fought this beast once before. He would never abandon anyone suffering from the same thing.

"That's what I thought."

Tobin's shoulders fell in defeat at Sergio's boast. He couldn't live with Sergio not having an out, though. "When you get tired, I won't hate you when you stop coming around. I'm your friend too. That means wanting you to be happy. No matter what. Even if I'm not in the picture."

Sergio held Tobin's waist and penguin-walked him toward the bedroom. "Don't get me wrong. Like, we'll be good pals and all, but I still plan to touch your dick. I hope you're not thinking I'm gonna be just some guy. We're still more than all that. You can count on me for other things than kicking it together —like I'll touch your naughty places and whatever."

Despite everything, a laugh burst from Tobin. He had no idea where this guy had come from. They barely knew each other and here Sergio was, talking about hanging in there through the worst time of Tobin's life and still wanting to be more. The guy really was an idiot. Tobin didn't even want to be with Tobin right now. Damn. He didn't know how to say no to Sergio. Tobin also didn't know if he wanted to.

AFTER MAKING TOBIN GET BACK IN BED, SERGIO stood in the kitchen staring at the food Tobin had bought. Tobin had gone out shopping for a meal for Sergio, even though he could barely function. That generosity of heart had Sergio claiming to be a fantastic cook, which wasn't true on any level. Now he genuinely didn't know what to do or where to start. His brain was kind of frozen.

"Are you okay?"

Exasperation nearly choked Sergio as Tobin reappeared in the kitchen. "Didn't I just put you to bed? Why are you up?"

Tobin's eyebrows rose. "Why are you staring at that food like you don't know where to start?"

Sergio refused to answer. He would watch a YouTube tutorial if he had to, but he wasn't admitting he didn't know what to do with any of the shit Tobin brought home.

Tobin shook his head. "I needed a drink. You don't know how to cook, do you?"

Fuck. Tobin could read minds. Sergio tried harder not to give anything away.

With a chuckle, Tobin moved to the fridge and found a bottle of water. After setting the bottle on the counter, Tobin grabbed a bar stool and dragged it into the kitchen. He sat. "Okay. I'm technically still resting. Find the salt and pepper on the spice rack."

As Sergio moved to do as told, he realized Tobin planned to direct while Sergio cooked. Sergio could live with that if Tobin stayed seated. He found the salt and pepper and set to work. Following Tobin's instructions was a lot less stressful than starting and stopping a video while trying to find ingredients he didn't know if Tobin even owned. Plus, Tobin was super patient and Sergio felt like he was learning something new. He only set the smoke alarm off twice while pan-searing the steaks. That felt like a win to Sergio. Hell, not burning down Damon's bar felt like a major score.

By the time Sergio finished, the meal didn't look like it had been prepared by a chef, but it still smelled good. He was pretty proud of himself. Plus, Sergio had learned something unexpected. He felt certain he could repeat what Tobin had shown him.

"Try it. You look so pleased with yourself that you should get the first bite."

He glanced Tobin's way. Tobin looked much better than he had when Sergio had shown up earlier. He also looked expectant—like he wanted to watch Sergio take the first bite. Sergio grabbed a knife and cut into the steak. As he popped the food into his mouth, he was ridiculously proud of himself. It was every bit as good as some of the five-star restaurants he visited.

"How is it?"

Instead of answering, Sergio cut Tobin a bite and fed him. He watched Tobin chew. It was funny to him that he found even that sexy. There was something about Tobin. Sergio felt good in his company—like they were best friends and had known each other their entire lives. His shoulders weren't tensed. Sergio couldn't recall the last time he didn't have to watch for daggers at his back.

Tobin nodded. "Very good. I'm impressed. You keep cooking like this, and I might have to keep you."

"Might?"

Tobin scrunched up his nose. "Maybe," he said, dragging out the word. "I know." He snapped his fingers, as if finding the word that he had been searching for. "Possibly."

Sergio set the fork aside. "Oh, I see. You're feeling better and want to play. I get it. My steak may or may not keep you around, huh?" Sergio invaded Tobin's space and placed several loud kisses on the side of Tobin's neck while Tobin fought to push him away, laughing.

"No. I didn't mean that. I'll keep you."

At Tobin's change of heart, Sergio massaged Tobin's thighs. His seduction turned genuine. He lightly tongued Tobin's neck. Tobin stopped trying to push him away. Instead, he encircled Sergio's neck and pulled him closer. His laughter turned to moans. Sergio had always been an oral person. He loved the way Tobin tasted. Sergio peeled away Tobin's shirt so he could sample even more of Tobin's skin. He tried to be gentle. It was impossible with Tobin making sounds like he was ready to come with Sergio only licking his nipples.

The thin workout shorts Tobin wore made it easy for Sergio to shove his hand inside. Tobin's fingernails dug into Sergio's shoulders as Sergio stroked him.

"I've never wanted anyone like I want you."

At Tobin's confession, Sergio bent and swallowed Tobin's cock. He could make Tobin want him even more.

"Oh my god. I swear I can feel your slight accent on my dick."

Sergio almost came in his jeans. Tobin had a way of going from sweet and innocent to sexual as fuck that drove Sergio wild. He loved it. Tobin made him feel powerful—like only he knew how to flip Tobin's switch. The louder Tobin's moans became, the harder Sergio worked at getting him off. He sucked and licked, giving Tobin everything he had. Tobin's muscles tensed. He pulled Sergio's hair so hard, Sergio's scalp stung. Cum filled Sergio's mouth. He swallowed. Sergio took his time finishing Tobin. He made sure he licked Tobin clean before fixing Tobin's clothes and stealing a sweet kiss.

Sergio fought hard to ignore his aching cock as he pulled away. Tobin's flushed face and the way his eyes were filled with emotion made it hard for Sergio to think about anything else. He had a bigger plan in mind. Sergio intended to lay siege to Tobin's heart. That meant temporary discomfort.

He backed up a step. "I'll fix your plate. Do you usually eat at the bar or in the living room since you don't have a dining room?"

Tobin molded against Sergio's back before he could get away. His arms encircled Sergio and his hand was inside Sergio's pants before he realized Tobin had undone his button and zipper. Sergio slapped his hands down on the countertop when his knees weakened. Tobin didn't hold back. In fact, he two-handed Sergio, massaging his balls and stroking. Sergio held his breath. His muscles locked up and Sergio squeezed his eyes closed, trying to hold back. He was too on edge from blowing Tobin. As if Tobin read his mind and knew he wasn't ready to come just yet, Tobin tightened his grip around the base of Sergio's cock and held still, cutting off Sergio's orgasm before it happened. Two steadying breaths past and Tobin pressed his lips to the spot between

Sergio's shoulder blades. It was the last sweet gesture Sergio got. Tobin pumped and stroked, making Sergio wild with lust. He openly fucked Tobin's hand. A half second before he blew, Sergio covered his cock with his shirt to keep from blowing all over Tobin's kitchen. Sergio swore he went blind for a second. It felt like he got hit by two orgasms at once. That was something that had never happened to him before. He barely kept his knees from collapsing as Tobin massaged every drop of cum from him.

"We should eat on the couch. It's more comfortable there."

Emotion choked Sergio at Tobin's offhand remark. He turned and captured Tobin's mouth. Sergio knew he really did need to let Tobin eat. The guy needed his strength, but Sergio recognized something monumental in that moment. He liked Tobin way more than he should in such a short time. Tobin made him feel good. No one else made Sergio feel good anymore. He always felt like he couldn't be himself because the world was watching. People used him and were always fake. Tobin felt different. It felt like Tobin actually cared. No one cared about him anymore. Tobin's attention was addicting. Sergio wanted more. He needed Tobin to be okay because he needed Tobin. As their tongues stroked, Sergio silently made a vow. He would fight for Tobin like no one else ever had before. Sergio wanted this thing they were starting. He wouldn't let anything endanger them. Tobin would see. He would keep Sergio.

FOUR

SERGIO SPENT every night at Tobin's place when he was in town. Oddly, Tobin's schedule of being up by three every morning had Sergio living the healthiest lifestyle he had in a long time. He liked helping Tobin box up his baked goods before heading out for a run each day. By the time he made it to scheduled practices, he was warmed up and ready to go. By eight every night, he was dead on his feet and ready for some cuddle time. He was happier than he could recall being at any point in his life.

Maybe that was why he was already awake fifteen minutes before the alarm and couldn't take his eyes off Tobin sleeping beside him. The tiny ball of determination curled up against him was quickly becoming his everything. Sometimes, from nowhere,

Sergio would get sideswiped by pure terror. His throat would threaten to close, and the shaking would set in. He had never been more afraid of losing anyone. Sergio had a dream career and more money than he had known existed as a kid. Despite those things, life hadn't been kind to him. While Sergio had been born in this country, his mom had been here illegally. She had sneaked across the border while pregnant with him to escape an abusive husband. When she had been diagnosed with breast cancer, she hadn't found many resources available to her. Not to mention, she had feared deportation.

Shortly after Sergio turned fourteen, Sergio's mom passed. She had instilled a healthy dose of fear of the system and authorities in him. So he had packed a bag, sold what he could, and grabbed all the funds he could get before landing in the streets. Sergio had lived in homeless camps and ran with thugs to stay alive. Meeting Valor had saved Sergio. With Valor's guidance, Sergio had learned how to use his talents to move up in the world. Sergio owed Valor everything for the lifestyle he now enjoyed. But inside, where no one could see, Sergio was still that kid who had lost his mom. He always seemed to fall for guys who used him just because they talked an excellent game. They made him believe he wouldn't go back to being alone. Before Tobin, Sergio had gotten a little jaded. Maybe he still was. But Tobin made him believe in love and Sergio might lose him the same way he had lost his mom. Life just kept sucker-punching him.

The alarm beeped and Tobin stirred. Sergio leaned past him and killed the sound so he could be the one who pulled Tobin from his dreams. He turned on the lamp by the bed before swiping his fingers down the line of Tobin's jaw.

Tobin smiled, but he didn't open his eyes. "Good morning."

Sergio bit his lip. Damn, he had it bad. "Good morning."

There were still black smudges beneath Tobin's eyes—like he never slept. Sergio lightly brushed his fingertips over the marks, wishing them away.

"I don't want to get up."

Tobin sounded genuinely exhausted and he still didn't open his eyes. Sergio found himself snuggling close and nuzzling Tobin's neck. He blew on Tobin's neck, making rude noises before kissing the same spot. "Don't worry, angel. I'll help you bake before I go for my run. You can stay in bed, if you want, and your customers will just get what they get from me— your baker in training."

With a soft laugh, Tobin pushed at his chest. "Fine. I'm getting up."

Sergio settled onto his back and linked his hands behind his head. He eyed Tobin's nude body as he pushed his way into sitting on the edge of the bed. Tobin was beautiful. Sergio loved staring at him. He was so tiny and angelic. Sergio wasn't a huge guy either, but he felt like Tobin would fit in his pocket.

Tobin chuckled. "I can feel you staring at me. I swear I'm moving." Tobin's words trailed off as he glanced over his shoulder. His smile slipped away. Before Sergio could ask what was wrong, Tobin picked up something from his pillow. It was a huge lock of hair. Tobin looked away. His shoulders dropped. Sergio's eyes fell closed. He swore he felt Tobin's pain. Tobin had adorable blond curls. They were soft, and Sergio loved running his fingers through them each time Tobin sucked him. Fuck. He hated this. The pain of a new loss radiated from Tobin. Sergio couldn't take it. He rolled from the bed and headed for the bathroom. Sergio flipped on the lights and started searching the cabinets.

"What are you looking for?"

As Tobin's question floated into the bathroom, Sergio found what he had been hunting. He quickly plugged in the electric razor, took one last look in the mirror, and buzzed through the center of his hair.

"Holy shit. What are you doing?" Tobin rushed inside the bathroom. He stopped dead in his tracks in the doorway. Tobin covered his mouth with both hands as Sergio took a second swipe through his hair. A horrified-sounding chuckle burst from behind Tobin's hands.

Sergio glanced over. "Don't laugh. You're next."

Tobin's eyes swam with laughter. His hands moved from his mouth to his cheeks. "You're insane."

"I've been called worse." Sergio made quick work of shaving his head. Once finished, he waved Tobin closer. "Your turn."

Tobin pulled a face but moved to stand in front of Sergio.

Sergio kissed Tobin's ear. "Good boy." With no mercy in his heart, and fast before he lost his courage, Sergio shaved Tobin's head. Tobin didn't make a sound, but he looked heartbroken when his hair was gone.

They stood together in silence in front of the mirror for much longer than necessary when it was done.

"It's for the best," Tobin said after a minute. His

tone didn't match his words. In fact, his voice cracked.

Sergio wrapped his arms around Tobin's chest and held on. He kissed Tobin's nape when Tobin's chin dropped. Sergio swore he could feel Tobin's heartbreak. "We're in this together," Sergio swore against Tobin's skin.

Tobin squeezed Sergio's arm across his chest but didn't lift his chin. "Where did you even come from? This is too much for me to ask from you." The words were barely a whisper, but Sergio heard each one. He refused to let Tobin use the moment to push him away.

"You're worth it. Let's get a shower and get to baking before you end up late." He didn't want to make a big deal out of shaving his head. At least he had a choice in the matter. Tobin didn't.

"Are you showering with me?"

Sergio snorted. "Hell yeah. Was there ever any doubt?"

With a laugh, Tobin stepped out of his hold and headed for the shower. Sergio took several deep breaths while Tobin got the water started. Every day, reality got a lot realer, and still Sergio couldn't walk away. Tobin glanced behind him. A small smile touched his lips and Sergio was hooked all over again. He would take however much time he could get with Tobin. Life wasn't guaranteed to anyone.

With that thought firm inside his mind, Sergio stripped and joined Tobin in the shower. They were lazy, taking their time washing each other. Sergio's chest filled with an unnamed emotion each time Tobin kissed his collarbone. Tobin's skin was pale against his. He fit perfectly in Sergio's arms. Sergio lingered over washing every inch of Tobin. By the time they stepped out of the shower, steam hung in the air. Tobin dried Sergio's skin with a fluffy towel. Each of Tobin's motions was slow and Sergio wasn't so sure that was due to lovingly caring for Sergio.

Sergio took the towel from Tobin. "I've got this. Go get dressed. I'm stealing too much of your time this morning." And energy, he silently added.

With one last kiss to Sergio's chest, Tobin did as told. Sergio kept one eye on Tobin as they dressed and brushed their teeth. When they moved to the kitchen, Sergio found himself sticking to Tobin's side, catching things as Tobin lost his strength to hold them. There was no missing the way his hands shook by the time the last batch of rolls was made.

"I need more boxes. I'll be right back."

Even though Sergio nodded, he really only half heard. His mind had fixated on the problem at hand

and wouldn't budge. Tobin did too much and that needed to stop. Between getting up at three to cook every morning, making deliveries all over town, going to chemo, and Sergio zapping his energy, there was no time left for Tobin to relax and heal. There had to be some way to make his life better. There had to be a better balance.

Sergio waited for what felt like ages for Tobin to return with the boxes, but Tobin didn't reappear. A hint of panic set in. He worried Tobin already thought he hovered too much. Still, he couldn't stand there any longer, waiting and fretting. Sergio glanced down the stairs leading to the storeroom. Tobin sat on the top step with his head leaned against the wall beside him, unmoving.

"Are you okay?" When Tobin didn't respond, Sergio rushed down a few steps to get a better look at Tobin. Silent tears streamed down Tobin's face. He looked defeated. Sergio instantly felt sick. Tobin's tears broke him.

"I can't do it."

Sergio tried not to show his inner panic at Tobin's whispered words. "You can't do what, *bebé?*"

Tobin sniffed. Even his voice sounded weak. "I can't make it down the stairs. I'm just so tired. Nothing works. I can't do it."

Sergio nodded. The huge knot in his throat made it hard for him to speak. He fought the fear choking him. Sergio was done trying to let Tobin be independent. He needed help. This had gone too far. "Don't move. Okay?"

Tobin nodded.

Sergio hurried down the stairs. He spotted Damon across the room as he pushed his way inside the bar.

Damon took one look at Sergio and straightened away from the table he had been polishing. "What's happened?"

"I need your help." Sergio didn't care about pride. "Tobin is sitting at the top of the stairs crying because he doesn't have the energy to make it down the steps."

Damon's eyes fell closed for a second, and Sergio knew he wasn't overreacting. His determination doubled. "He can't keep working anymore. What he has scheduled for today is mostly ready to go out, but he can't do it. I want to take him home with me. He needs to focus on getting better. As long as he has to fight so hard to survive financially, he won't stop until he kills himself. I can't let that happen."

Damon nodded. "I agree." He glanced around as if trying to think over the situation. "I have a beer delivery coming this morning. Otherwise, I would offer to make his deliveries for him today. That way, you could go ahead and take him home. I don't know what to do about that."

"I'll stay and wait for the beer guy."

Sergio spun. A guy with dark hair and perfect lips sat at a table nearby. Sergio hadn't realized they weren't alone. His ink-colored straight hair hung in his eyes, making them seem even lighter by comparison. Sergio found himself blinking against the sight of the guy. It was unnatural for one person to be so flawless. In fact, it was almost off-putting— like something about the guy was fake.

Damon growled. The aggravation in the sound couldn't be missed. "I guess—if you're willing—I don't have any other choice."

The guy smiled. It was slow and evil-looking— like he relished the idea of forcing Damon into his debt. "It seems you don't."

Sergio didn't have the luxury of caring what the dynamic was between the pair or why the guy was drinking alone this early in the morning in a closed bar. He was scared shitless he would find Tobin at the bottom of the steps if he didn't hurry.

Damon tossed his hand towel onto the table. "Let's go. I'll make Tobin's deliveries and inform all his customers that it might be awhile before he's well enough to continue. You get Tobin in the car before he regains enough strength to fight you. He's stubborn like that."

Damon headed toward the door leading to the steps. He came to a sudden stop before turning back the lone customer's way. "Oh, Lucky, before I forget. The delivery guy will be here in like thirty. You just need to unlock the back door and sign for the beer." His jaw flexed and Sergio swore his eye twitched. "Thank you." Damon sounded as if he choked on the words before quickly turning away.

An unmistakable soft and evil-sounding chuckle followed them to the door. Sergio had no idea what was going on there, but it was obvious the two had issues. He didn't care about that. Sergio didn't care about anything except Tobin. It was time to overstep his bounds.

IT SCARED TOBIN HOW MUCH HE HAD COME TO depend on seeing Sergio's face in the few short weeks they had been dating. He hadn't intended to meet such an amazing man, especially at this point in his life. Here he was, nonetheless. Tobin couldn't get enough of Sergio's teasing smiles and overall amazingness. Unfortunately, Tobin's body didn't care that his soul had connected with someone. It ached.

Tobin felt sick to his stomach and his entire body shook with weakness. Invisible sandbags weighed him down. Tobin sat in the stairwell, bald and wanting to die. He couldn't do this. There was such a long battle ahead of him, and he already felt too bad to move. He wouldn't survive this. It was best he passed now. The months of suffering left to go looked unending. He could already see the days stretching out into a bleak future. Every day he would wake at three to keep going through the motions, only to end up here, sitting at the top of the steps unable to make the descent. Tobin had no other choice. He couldn't afford to stop working. Yet he didn't have the energy to keep going. His life was over. He kind of wished it would just end already.

Damon and Tobin appeared at the bottom of the stairs, looking determined.

Damon motioned Tobin's way. "You get him, and I'll pack him a bag. I'll bring the rest of his things by tonight after I make his deliveries and my nightshift guys come in."

"Sounds good," Sergio said as he jogged up the

steps. Sergio made soothing noises as he swept Tobin into his arms. "Come on, sweetie. You're going home with me for a while."

Tobin couldn't stop the tears leaking from his eyes. He had never been much of a crier, but that was all he felt like doing anymore. "I can't. All my things for work are here. I have deliveries to honor."

Sergio's features hardened, but his tone stayed comforting. "Work is over for you for now. Damon will make today's deliveries and let all your clients know what's going on. It's time to focus on your health."

Tobin cried harder. Everything was slipping away. "I can't do that. I have medical bills and rent to pay."

"Fuck your bills," Damon said as he opened the front door so Sergio could carry Tobin out to the car. "I'll survive without your rent money. The same can't be said of losing you. You need to get better. You're all I have left, and you fucking know it, so you can't die. I won't let you."

Sergio didn't even bother arguing or discussing things with Tobin the way Damon did. He simply strapped Tobin into the front seat of his car like a child. Tobin couldn't fight. His strength was gone. He stared at his lap, defeated.

"Look at me."

Tobin glanced over at Sergio's demand. He was stooped next to Tobin's open door, waiting for Tobin's attention. He looked unmoving and beautiful.

Once Sergio had Tobin's attention, he made the tears worse. "I have you. Do you feel me? I've got your back. You can be angry or feel guilty—whatever you want—later. Right now, you need to stop and look at me. Do I look like I'm giving you a choice?"

Tobin shook his head. Sergio truly looked dead set in this decision.

Sergio gave him a sharp nod. A slight smile touched Sergio's lips. "You're being abducted. It isn't your fault that I've decided to keep you. Is there anything you can do about it?"

Tobin shook his head again. If he couldn't walk down a set of stairs, there was no way he could stop Sergio from kidnapping him.

Sergio pushed to his feet and kissed Tobin's forehead. "Exactly." He peeled off his shirt and used it to wipe Tobin's face. "Ain't shit happening to you on my watch. Hang on to this."

Tobin clasped the shirt Sergio handed him to his chest. He tried to come to terms with reality as Sergio talked to Damon. Damon handed him a duffle bag. They shook hands before parting ways. Sergio opened the car's hatch and tossed the bag inside before climbing behind the wheel. All Tobin could do was stare at him in shocked silence. This was really happening. Sergio was right. There was nothing Tobin could do. Sergio was in charge now. Tobin was too weak to fight.

By the time they made it to Sergio's, Tobin tears had dried away and his hands no longer shook. Unfortunately, that was mostly due to his inability to stay awake. Sergio had a gorgeous house. It wasn't an estate like Reid's place, but it was definitely a mansion. The place had two pools. One inside and one outside. Thankfully, there was an elevator because Tobin wanted to walk but steps were too much. Still, by the time they made it from the garage, through the vast house, and inside Sergio's bedroom, Tobin was leaning on Sergio with more weight than not.

At the edge of the bed, Sergio stripped him to his underwear. "You're so beautiful."

Tobin wanted to call bullshit. There was no way he looked anything but terrible at the moment. He was too tired to argue.

Sergio helped him into bed, then started stripping.

Tobin's guilt doubled. "What are you doing? You haven't been for your morning run or anything."

Sergio shushed him as he climbed in bed with Tobin. "Everything can wait a little while longer. I don't really have anything to do until practice this afternoon. Right now, I need to hold you while you sleep."

Tobin wanted to cry again, but he didn't have the energy. "This isn't fair. You deserve better than me. Please don't do this to yourself. Just take me home and let me go."

"Shut up before you piss me off with that crazy talk." Sergio roughly gathered Tobin into his arms. He kissed Tobin's ear. "Don't say any of that dumbass shit to me again. Promise me."

Tobin closed his eyes and took a breath. He fought the urge to continue trying to convince Sergio to walk away. Sergio had his entire life ahead of him. Tobin didn't want to watch Sergio grow to resent him, but Sergio sounded truly angry. Tobin cared too much to fight. "I promise." Even as he said the words Sergio wanted to hear, Tobin's heart couldn't take it. He rolled in Sergio's arms and buried his face in the crook of Sergio's neck. The shock had somewhat worn off enough for Tobin to realize his current position. Sergio had brought him home to care for him. Who did something like that after like a month of dating? Sergio had shaved his head and planned to take care of Tobin—like an insane superhero. Tobin couldn't wrap his mind around it. He was so blown away that he didn't know what to say. Tobin wanted to leave and save Sergio from himself, but he couldn't. He felt guilty as hell and moved beyond words. Tobin had never been backed by anyone in his life like this. He didn't understand.

"Why are you doing this?"

Sergio stroked his back and comforted him. "Because you're worth it and I like being with you." With his face pressed to Sergio's throat, Tobin felt Sergio swallow. He held Tobin a little tighter. "I can't live with knowing anything bad is happening to you. You matter to me. So let me have this, okay? Maybe it'll be your turn someday to take care of me. Until then, I need to do this. I need to make you better."

Tobin's muscles relaxed. He didn't feel so much like the intruder after Sergio's explanation. Maybe he wanted Sergio to make it easier for him to be a burden and grasped at the first explanation he got. Tobin wanted to be important to Sergio. He wanted to live so they could have a life together.

"I'll get better quick."

A soft chuckle rumbled from Sergio's chest. "You

really sounded like you could will yourself into being healed just then. That's the part of you I can't resist." Sergio urged Tobin's chin up and held Tobin's stare. "I know I'm too much for most people, but not you. You have no clue how much you give me by letting me be myself. I think you should kiss me before you pass out."

Tobin didn't hesitate to scoot higher and claim Sergio's lips. His whole life he had been told if something sounded too good to be true, then it probably was. That had always held true until now. For once, Tobin really believed Sergio was exactly who he presented. Tobin needed it to be real. In the midst of a horrible existence, Sergio looked like a rainbow sent from above. Tobin couldn't think Sergio was anything less than a blessing. He would sleep the day away and gather his strength. Tobin would get better, because there was no way in hell he would miss out on a life with this guy. Fuck cancer. Tobin had a future waiting for him.

FIVE

TWO MONTHS of living with Sergio had Tobin feeling way better than he had in a long time. He still got tired easily, but when he felt the exhaustion hit, nothing stopped him from going to bed. Tobin still felt guilty as hell all the time. Sergio paid all his bills and Damon kept Tobin on his insurance at the bar in a deal they had worked out a long time ago. Tobin wasn't pulling his weight in any relationship in his life, but he still tried. Anytime he felt good enough, he still made his rolls for a few places and he visited his friends whenever he could. Most of the time, he dedicated his energy to making Sergio's life easier while focusing on his health. He couldn't get enough of the man who had swept into his life like a knight. There was nothing normal about the way their relationship started. It was like they had been in overdrive, grabbing at all the minutes they could get before Tobin's time ran out. Tobin had no regrets about the fast pace. Bad timing aside, he had met the one. Hopefully, he still felt the same after tonight.

"Up next, our Stassie Davidson talks with Sergio Costa about the Lancers' winning season."

Tobin turned away from the stove to stare at the TV built into the fridge door. Sergio was on his way home, so anyone talking with Sergio had to have been recorded earlier in the day. Still, Tobin had to watch. He still had a hard time wrapping his mind around Sergio's fame. Sergio didn't act like a man who lived in a multi-million-dollar house, drove an expensive car, and had countless fans. He was just Sergio. Tobin would never understand what Sergio saw in him, but Tobin wasn't dumb enough to turn away from someone so amazing.

The long-haired brunette who covered sports on their local station appeared on the screen. Sergio stood at her side on the soccer field. He was sweaty and Tobin's mouth watered with a sudden desire to lick him. Tobin couldn't get enough. He had to force himself to pay attention to the interview.

"There's no denying the Lancers are having a great season, and a big reason for the team's success is standing right here." She turned Sergio's way. "So, Sergio, everyone knows you're having a phenomenal year, and while I have lots of questions that I want to ask about your stats, everyone I've spoken to lately has just one question they need answered. What happened to your hair? Is the heat getting to you?"

A chuckle escaped Tobin. He covered his mouth to stifle the sound, even though he was alone. It sounded evil and seemed wrong to laugh at Sergio being put on the spot.

The infectious smile Tobin loved so much made an appearance at the reporter's question. Tobin bit back a sigh. Sergio had one of those boyish grins that drew people in. "I'm never bothered by the heat," Sergio argued in mock offense. He turned serious before the reporter could apologize. "Actually, my boyfriend is battling leukemia and I've been shaving my hair for him. We're in this fight together and my hair will stay this way until he gets his back."

The back door beeped, letting Tobin know Sergio was home. Tobin quickly turned off the TV before Sergio caught him watching the interview. He turned away and stirred the dinner he had been cooking when Sergio's name had caught his attention. Even Tobin didn't know why he didn't want Sergio to know he had seen, but it felt like he was too obsessed—like he stalked Sergio when they were apart.

Sergio tossed his keys on the kitchen counter before invading Tobin's space. He kissed the side of Tobin's neck. "Something smells good. How is my sexy *bebé* doing today?"

"I'm good. I just saw you on the news." Damn, he was always telling on himself.

"Mhmm," Sergio hummed against Tobin's nape as he kept kissing every inch of bare skin above Tobin's collar.

Tobin drew a ragged breath. Now wasn't the time to get turned on. "Um." He tried to rub two coherent thoughts together with Sergio touching him. "I have some news you may not love."

Sergio froze. Tobin swore he felt Sergio's every muscle tense. "Is everything okay?"

"Of course." Tobin realized too late he might have scared Sergio with his dire tone. He set his spoon aside and turned in Sergio's arms. "It's just that I've barely been holding my parents at bay since I moved in, and my mom has had enough. She sort of demanded to visit. So I said they could come to dinner." Tobin winced as the final words fell from his lips. They hadn't talked about Sergio meeting Tobin's family yet. Tobin truly hadn't been left a choice. His mom was the type to call the police and report him as missing if he didn't cooperate.

Sergio shrugged. "That's fine. This is your home. Of course they're welcome here."

Tobin chewed his bottom lip. Sergio sounded fine, but he hadn't met them yet. "Are you sure? We haven't really talked about you meeting them... or anything, really."

As Sergio dragged Tobin closer, he cocked his head to one side and eyed Tobin. "What's going on in your head?"

Heat crawled up Tobin's cheeks. He hated being put on the spot. Inside, he squirmed with discomfort. "I mean, like they have questions about us. They want to know how long this has been going on and where it's headed. My parents won't likely keep those questions to themselves. I don't know how to answer because we've never actually talked about it either."

Sergio stared at Tobin's lips. "Damn, *bebé*. I'm sorry. You're so sexy. I didn't really catch a word of that. All I can think about is this." He swooped in and claimed Tobin's mouth. As always, Sergio's kiss was mind-blowing. It was impossible to think with Sergio's tongue in his mouth. If they had been having an important discussion, Tobin lost the threads. He was in love with this man. Every day, Tobin came to grips with that reality a little more. Sergio was always there, being supportive and perfect. They spent every moment Sergio wasn't out of town or doing work stuff together. There had never really been any adjustment period or a need for one. They just clicked and fit. Sergio didn't have any annoying habits Tobin couldn't handle. If Tobin had any Sergio couldn't take, he never said anything. They were happy. Sometimes Tobin forgot to be afraid, and that mattered.

The doorbell sounded through the house just as Sergio backed Tobin against the counter, as if he planned to fuck him right there.

Sergio lifted his head. His cheeks were flushed and his eyes hooded. He stared down at Tobin with swollen lips and lust in his eyes. Tobin could barely breathe. Words he feared saying stuck in his throat. Emotion weighed heavy on his chest.

"I'm guessing that's your parents."

Tobin blinked. Reality came crashing back. Soon, they wouldn't be alone. "Shit."

A smile exploded across Sergio's face. "I take that as a yes."

It would be a few hours before they were alone again. Maybe that was a good thing. Sometimes

Tobin scared himself when it came to Sergio. He had never felt this way about anyone. Tobin didn't want to send Sergio running for the hills with his intensity. But damn, he wanted to keep Sergio for good. He had to keep reminding himself this arrangement was temporary. As soon as he was well enough to go home, he would. Tobin couldn't let himself get too comfortable in this relationship. Sergio was only helping him through the worst. He likely wouldn't want to be tied to this forever. Tobin always needed to keep that at the forefront of his mind. He was a charity case. Tobin couldn't forget it.

SERGIO COULD BEND STEEL WITH HIS DICK. Something about coming home to Tobin always hit him right in the gut. He loved the sight of Tobin, looking rested and at home under Sergio's roof, and it really got to him. It was like they were a family. Sergio hadn't lived this life since he was little. His house felt filled with love and Sergio couldn't get enough. Then there was the way Tobin looked at him—like he had come home. Goddamn, Tobin made him realize he had never been in love before

Tobin came into his life. Sergio had never felt this much for anyone—like he would kill to keep Tobin.

The funny thing was, though, Sergio didn't really think about where they were headed until Tobin's parents walked through the door. Tobin was a perfect mixture of Janet and Bill. He had Bill's blond hair and Janet's green eyes. Janet's nose and Bill's smile. Sergio liked them on sight, as if he couldn't dislike anyone who shared Tobin's blood and features. Plus, they were genuinely nice.

Janet had stepped right into his space and fussed over him like a mom. She hugged him and gave him a ton of compliments before grabbing his hand and turning Tobin's way. "Oh my goodness. He's so handsome. I'm sure you have a terrible time keeping your hands to yourself."

Tobin blushed.

Sergio tried not to laugh, but he refused to pretend he couldn't hear her loudly talking about him. "Thank you."

Janet met his gaze again. "No. Thank you. I hear you've been taking care of my son. Damon has had nothing but good things to say about you. I'd love to meet your mom so I can tell her what an amazing job she did with you."

Sergio's smile faltered. "She passed when I was fourteen."

"I'm so sorry." Janet pressed her hand to her chest. "That breaks my heart. Well, you're a member of our family for life now. I don't know how you convinced Tobin to let you take care of him, but I'll never forget it."

Before he could stop it from happening, Sergio snorted. "He didn't let me. I stole him and took over his life. He's kind of a willing captive at this point."

Janet eyes looked so much like Tobin's, and they swam with laughter. Sergio couldn't look away. "That's the only way Tobin has ever made friends. Do you know, that's how we got Damon as part of our family? Tobin's car broke down and Damon stopped to help. Even though Tobin's phone was dead, and he was twenty minutes from anything, he wouldn't let Damon help. Damon finally yelled at him to get in his goddamn car so he could take him to his momma." Janet laughed at her own story. "He was only sixteen, so I was furious he had gotten in the car with a stranger, but also so, so thankful it was Damon who stopped to help—like he had been sent by an angel. I have to think the same of you. Tobin won't let anyone do anything for him. He's way too determined to face life alone. I don't know why. It's always been that way. Even as a little boy, he always refused help with anything. He used to fight me to hold his own bottle and even tried changing his own diapers—like just frustrating as hell his whole life." Janet crossed the room and squeezed Tobin to her chest. "But he's my baby."

Tobin didn't pull away or seem embarrassed by his mom's affection or stories. In fact, he leaned into her and wrapped his arms around her—like he wasn't the least bit ashamed of loving her. In that moment, Sergio understood Tobin better than he ever had. Tobin wasn't stubborn. He loved hard and didn't want to burden the people he loved in any way. It wasn't hardheadedness. Tobin wanted to make life easier for everyone else by taking on all life's hardships alone. Each new detail he gathered about Tobin made Sergio's respect grow. Tobin was more amazing than anyone Sergio had ever met. He deserved to be surrounded by people who loved him just as much.

Bill moved to stand next to him, cutting into Sergio's thoughts. He patted Sergio's shoulder. Bill kept his voice low and their conversation private while Janet stole all the hugs from Tobin. "Like Janet said, we genuinely appreciate everything you're doing. Tobin won't let us help, and that's killing his mom. Knowing that he's let someone in is the only thing keeping her sane through this."

Sergio nodded. He felt warm all over and couldn't explain why. "It's no problem. Really." An overwhelming need to say something and make Tobin's parents feel even more secure about Tobin's care rose to the surface. "He's my boy. I have to be there for this." Sergio knew he wasn't doing a good job of explaining himself, but he didn't know how to talk about his feelings, especially to parents. Valor was the only person to pull words from Sergio when it came to the heart, but Valor was like his dad or something similar. Bill was a stranger, except he was Tobin's dad, and that hit Sergio in the feels. "I love him."

Bill squeezed his shoulder. "It's good to hear that. Nothing will make us less scared, but it matters a lot that you're with him, especially since he had declined treatment when he first found out. It killed us inside that he had chosen to die rather than endure chemo again, but we couldn't convince him to change his mind. Then, out of the blue about three months ago, he said he would fight. I don't know if you had anything to do with him changing his mind, but we're grateful nonetheless. We can't lose our son."

Sergio's throat swelled as he watched Janet placing loud kisses on Tobin's cheek until he laughed. They were an adorable family. After watching Tobin suffer these past few months, Sergio understood Tobin not wanting to do this twice in one life. Sergio could also understand Tobin not wanting to drag his parents through the ugliness of chemo and the days he was too weak to move. That was fine. Sergio had him. He wouldn't let Tobin give up. That wasn't happening on his watch.

"I can't either," Sergio said more for himself. As long as there was life left in Sergio's chest, he would keep Tobin alive. Nothing would stand in his way.

———

By the time Tobin's parents left, he was exhausted. Tobin only had enough energy left for a shower and then he was back in bed. No one knew how much he fucking hated being trapped in a body that wouldn't do everything his mind still wanted to do. Sergio had been amazing with his parents. Of course, Sergio was always fantastic. Tobin just wished he could be equally great in Sergio's eyes, but his body always held him back.

Sergio climbed into bed and settled onto his side

next to Tobin. They held each other's stare. Tobin didn't know who reached out first, but their fingers met and linked. A smile tugged at Tobin's lips.

"Thank you for today. I know Mom and Dad are overwhelming."

"Nope. You're lucky they're still around to wear you down. They're welcome here anytime. This is your home. You're allowed to invite people to visit."

Tobin avoided that last bit because he still felt strange about camping out at Sergio's. "What were your parents like?"

Sergio lifted one shoulder in a half shrug. "My mom never talked about my dad other than to say he was an abusive ass, and I was too stubborn to ask more. I thought I had my whole life to get over being angry at him. But then she was gone and there was no one left to ask. Mom was... legit crazy," Sergio said with a laugh. "She was always loud. That was her way of keeping me out of trouble. If she saw me acting too big, she would get loud-mouthed and embarrassing. She would turn bright—like singsong as she followed me all the way to the door of the school, yelling how much she loved her big boy. It was embarrassing as shit." Sergio's smile slipped away. "I miss her." For a moment, Sergio seemed to stare at nothing, seeing only what went on inside his head. Tobin's chest ached while he stared at Sergio. He wished he could give her back. Finally, Sergio blinked and focused on Tobin again. "Your dad said you declined treatment when you first found out."

Tobin winced but didn't respond. There was nothing to say. He wished his dad hadn't told that to Sergio.

When he didn't speak, Sergio pressed on. "He also said you changed your mind three months ago... around the time we started dating. What made you decide to start treatment?"

Tobin shrugged, feeling exposed. He could feel the heat climbing up his cheeks and he prayed his face wasn't as red as it felt. "Does it matter?"

"Yes." Sergio scooted closer. He urged Tobin to drape one leg over his hip so he could get even closer. "It matters to me. Choosing to die is a fucking huge commitment. It had to take something just as big to change your mind."

Tobin drew a shaky breath. He could tell by the way Sergio looked at him that Sergio wouldn't let this go. Tobin chose to be honest, even though it was humiliating. "It was kind of an epiphany. I was sitting in the middle of Reid and Valor's engagement party and reality sort of slammed into me. In that moment, I realized I would never have that. Of all the things I haven't gotten to do or experience, that was the one thing I regretted more than never traveling or anything else."

"An engagement party?"

Tobin shook his head. "Not getting to fall in love and having someone look at me the way Valor looks at Reid. I regret that the most." Tobin swallowed, wondering if he should stop. Sergio looked as if he held his breath and Tobin kept going, even though his voice turned quieter by the second. "Then you walked in the door and looked my way. Suddenly, I wasn't quite so ready to die. I realized I had at least one more thing I wanted from this life."

Sergio's gaze hooded as he inched even closer. His hand found its way inside the back of Tobin's shorts. He stroked Tobin's ass as the air around them grew heavier with desire. "Have you finished scratching me off your to-do list?"

Tobin shook his head. His hand slid across Sergio's waist. "Not yet."

"Good." Somehow, Sergio's expression turned hotter. "You'd better have my name written in permanent ink on that list. Fuck, tattooed on it."

"Should I?" Tobin couldn't stop the teasing note in his voice.

Sergio nodded. "If you haven't noticed, you have

someone who looks at you the way Valor looks at Reid. Is that all you wanted? Because I don't want to stop at a look."

The space between them got smaller by the second. Their lips nearly brushed. Tobin's eyes slipped closed. "That's not all I want."

"Tell me what you want," Sergio demanded on a whisper.

Held captive by the spell Sergio weaved, Tobin confessed his deepest secret. "Your heart. Forever."

"Done." Sergio overcame Tobin as the single word left his lips. Tobin swore he tasted the promise on Sergio's tongue. On his back, with Sergio straddling his body, Tobin believed in that moment like never before that he had—by some miracle—stolen Sergio's heart. The instant that reality sank in, Tobin made another discovery. Sergio couldn't be scratched off his list. He was the paper the list was written upon. Everything Tobin wanted to do before he died, he wanted to do with Sergio. Right now, he craved feeling Sergio's skin against his.

Tobin pushed Sergio's pajama pants down until Sergio's erection sprang free. A happy hum escaped him as he wrapped his fingers around Sergio's cock. "Mine."

"That was so possessive and adorable coming

from you," Sergio said with a chuckle as he worked on peeling Tobin's shorts down just enough to let him play with Tobin's dick.

A tiny mewling sound fell from Tobin's lips as Sergio stroked him. Sergio pushed Tobin's hand aside and reclaimed Tobin's mouth. Before Tobin had time to be disappointed over Sergio stealing his toy, Sergio moved against him. Their cocks massaged each other. Tobin gasped. Sergio changed angles and set a pace that had Tobin scratching at Sergio's skin while their tongues fought. Sergio did all the work. All Tobin could do was relax and get pleasured. Sergio was a master at keeping their relationship strong while Tobin still got the rest he needed. If Sergio felt neglected or like they were lacking in any way, he never showed it. Right now, they felt hotter than most relationships ever became.

Tobin's cock throbbed as pressure climbed his shaft. He tore his mouth away and gasped for air, straining for release.

Sergio licked his ear. "That's it, *bebé*. I want that hot cum all over my dick. You have no idea how hard I had to fight to keep my hands off you all night. I wanted to set your ass in the middle of my spaghetti, then eat it off your skin. Fuck, I can't function from wanting you. Let me have that cum."

A chant roared in Tobin's mind. Before he could stop it, the words fell from his lips. "Please. I love you. Please."

A roar sounded against Tobin's ear as Sergio came. The sound sent Tobin over the edge. His entire body shook with waves of ecstasy. Sergio grabbed his jaw and held tight as he reclaimed Tobin's mouth. "I love you too," Sergio whispered between kisses. Tobin felt a tear slip from the corner of his eye and roll back into his hair. He never expected Sergio. Yet here he was. For the first time in his life, he believed in a higher power. He felt blessed —like someone had intervened to save him right when he had given up. Tobin would cherish Sergio for all the days he was given. He knew a miracle when he saw one. Sergio was one hundred percent Tobin's savior. Tobin would love him forever.

SIX

TOBIN: *Doctor's appointment went good today. Numbers look great. I'm feeling halfway human. Maybe I can come to the game Monday?*

Sergio: *Did your doctor give the green light for that?*

Tobin: ***sad face** I didn't think to ask.*

Sergio: *I would feel better if you waited until he said it was okay. Miss you.*

Tobin: *I miss you too. I'm ready for you to come home.*

Sergio: *Three more days and I'll be there. I'm so tired. There's nothing I want more than to be with you.*

Tobin: *I know. Stay safe.*

TOBIN: OKAY. THE DOCTOR SAID, IF I WEAR A *mask, I can go to your next game. Yay!*

Sergio: *Do you really want to suffocate in a mask while watching something that bores the hell out of you?*

Tobin: *Yes. Besides, I'm not bored when you're playing. I like staring at your ass.*

Sergio: *Can we compromise?*

Tobin: *I suppose...*

Sergio: *If someone will come with you, in case you need to leave, then that's fine with me. I'll be stuck there, but you shouldn't be. Will that work?*

Tobin: *Yes. Yay.*

Sergio: *Someone has to come. Someone who will make you leave if you start feeling bad.*

Tobin: *I'll bring Damon. He'll take charge.*

Sergio: *Okay. I love you and I want you there, but not at the risk of your health.*

Tobin: *I love you too. I'll be good. Cross my heart.*

TOBIN: REID IS HERE TO KIDNAP ME FOR COFFEE AT *The Back Porch. I don't really want to go, but I also kind of do. He's my friend and I also don't want to lose my contacts for the business.*

Sergio: *Go. Have fun. Practice is running late tonight anyhow. Coach is riding our asses after yesterday's loss. It's all good.*

Tobin: *Okay. Love you.*

Sergio: *I love you too.*

SINCE SERGIO HAD NO FAMILY, HIS FAMILY dynamic was a bit odd. As a teenager living on the streets, Sergio had played sports with Valor—a local cop. Normally, Sergio wouldn't have messed with any type of law man. Valor was different, though. He didn't fake concern. For whatever reason, Valor genuinely cared and wanted Sergio to have a good life. He was the reason Sergio had made it big and Valor was his dad in Sergio's eyes. Valor being a father figure meant that another guy Valor had saved —Dawson—was kind of like a brother to Sergio. Dawson and he weren't as close as Sergio felt to Valor, but today, Sergio appreciated Dawson more than words. Without him, Sergio might have been crawling out of his skin with nerves.

Dawson squeezed his shoulder. "Don't worry, man. You've got this."

Sergio did not in fact have this, but he was trying. "Sure."

Dawson's eyes lit with humor, as if he could read Sergio's mind. "Seriously, Sergio. Go with your gut. It'll never lead you wrong. I've known my entire life that Milo was the one for me. When you know, you know." Dawson's gaze slid past Sergio. He nodded toward the small round window behind Sergio. "He's here."

Sergio turned and stepped to the side, ensuring Tobin didn't catch sight of him. He had been planning this moment since the day he met Tobin's parents three months ago. Soccer season was winding down and Tobin was getting out more. Sergio could practically feel Tobin getting restless and ready to move on. Tobin had already started dropping hints about getting back to work, which meant moving back to his apartment. Sergio couldn't have that. He had to convince Tobin to stay.

Wrecker led Tobin and Reid to a table near the back. Even from a distance, Sergio could make out every detail of Tobin's face. Since the day they met, he hadn't been able to get enough. Forever wouldn't be long enough with Tobin. He genuinely couldn't let Tobin move out. Each time Sergio left for practice or went out of town for a game, he spent the whole time scared shitless Tobin would decide he could live without Sergio and leave. No one understood how terrified Sergio was of being abandoned. Every time he loved someone, he lost them in some fashion. He couldn't lose Tobin. That wasn't an option. He had to lock him down.

Valor slipped through the back door of the coffeehouse with Bill and Janet. Bill gave him a thumbs-up, and as a group, they headed inside the dining area.

Sergio kept one eye on Tobin as he headed for the stage Wrecker had set up for the Wednesday night talent showcase The Back Porch held each week. Reid kept Tobin distracted until Sergio stepped up to the microphone and the entire shop fell silent. Wrecker nodded to let Sergio know the microphone was hot.

Sergio took a breath and dove in. "Hey everyone. Tonight's talent showcase doesn't start for a few more hours, but Wrecker is letting me take over the stage for a few minutes."

Tobin's head shot up and his gaze locked on Sergio. A deep line appeared between his eyebrows.

Oddly, Tobin's confusion over Sergio's presence

fed Sergio's confidence. "It's taken me a few months to get everyone I care about under the same roof, but with a bit of planning and deceit, I managed to pull it off. Don't worry. I won't take up a tremendous amount of your time. I just wanted everyone here so they could be a part of this. Tobin, I love you."

A smile snapped to Tobin's lips and a blush touched his cheeks. "I love you too."

Tobin's yelled words made several people laugh. Maybe Tobin had no clue what was going on, but he didn't let Sergio down by not playing along.

Sergio held Tobin's stare and leaned close to the microphone. "Do you love me enough to marry me?"

Tobin's smile grew. "Are you fucking kidding me?"

A laugh burst from Sergio at Tobin's response. "No pressure."

"Don't be an idiot. Of course I want to marry you."

Laughter and loud clapping filled the air as Sergio jumped down from the short stage and crossed the room. He pulled the ring he had bought from his pocket as he overcame Tobin. Uncaring of who watched, Sergio claimed Tobin's mouth while whistles sounded around them. Sergio pulled away and then buried his face against the crook of Tobin's neck. He kept his words for Tobin alone. "I realized too late how much I put you on the spot. If you want to say no, I understand."

Tobin lightly punched him in the ribs. "Give me my ring."

With a laugh, Sergio pulled away and slipped the ring on Tobin's finger. Tobin's eyes swam with happiness as he stared down at the gold band encircled with diamonds. "Oh my god. I can't believe you did this." He glanced around. "Holy shit. Everyone is here. My parents and Damon." Tobin pinned Reid with an accusing look. "Were you part of this?"

Reid's blue eyes showed his humor over Tobin's shock. He held his hands up in surrender. "It was the good kind of deceit."

Bill and Janet crowded around them, taking turns hugging Tobin and Sergio. Everyone followed Tobin's parents, congratulating them. Damon spoke quietly against Tobin's ear. Tobin blinked back tears and Damon turned away fast, as if he too had been overcome by emotion. Every second that passed, the realer everything felt. Sergio couldn't believe Tobin really planned to marry him. He couldn't believe his luck.

The more Sergio's happiness grew and the

longer he stared at Tobin, the more Sergio wished he had done this privately. Tobin deserved to be publicly celebrated, but Sergio wanted him alone now that the adrenaline had faded and reality set in. Tobin truly had agreed to marry him. The guy who hated crowds and leaving the house endured the attention now for Sergio. Sergio's throat swelled.

As if he felt Sergio's sudden surge of overwhelming emotions, Tobin found his hand. As their fingers linked, Tobin's gaze found his. The way Tobin's mouth lifted in one corner made Sergio feel as if Tobin read his mind. "I'm thinking I feel a bit tired and overwhelmed."

A smile snapped to Sergio's lips. They really were the perfect team. He wasted no time thanking everyone for being a part of their engagement and explaining that Tobin needed his rest. They made dinner plans with Tobin's parents and Valor and Reid. In under an hour, he had Tobin shuffled into the car. The moment they were closed inside, Tobin tried crawling into Sergio's lap.

Tobin kissed him deep before pulling away and pressing his forehead against Sergio's. Up close, Tobin's light green eyes seemed ever lighter. Sergio was happier than he had ever been in his life. Tobin's eyes crinkled in the corners. "There's still time to get away from me."

Sergio snorted. "I'm the one who asked you to marry me. I definitely don't want out."

Tobin settled down in his seat and looked at his ring. "I can't believe you did this."

"I can't believe you said yes."

Tobin rolled his eyes.

"We should get married right now."

Tobin laughed at Sergio's enthusiasm. "I would marry you in a heartbeat, baby, but take a breath. My mom would be really upset if she didn't get to be involved, and maybe I want a real wedding."

Sergio forced his excitement to take a step back. Tobin deserved a real wedding. Not only that, but once Tobin said the words, Sergio realized he wanted one too. He planned to only do this once. They should create memories with the best wedding ever. Still, there was also a small part of Sergio that wanted to marry right then before he lost his chance. He was torn.

Tobin's smile slipped away as his gaze moved over Sergio's face. "Okay."

Sergio blinked. "Okay, what?"

"Let's go get married right now."

Guilt washed over Sergio, but not for the right

things. He should have felt terrible for taking away the one thing Tobin requested. Instead, he felt bad for the amount of relief he felt over Tobin giving in. "Let's do both." The words burst from Sergio to assuage his shame. "Let's get married now and then have a big wedding whenever you're up to it."

"No. You're right. I probably can't handle the stress of a big wedding and it'll likely be a long time before I am well enough for that. If getting married is about being married, and you're ready, then we should just do it."

Sergio bit his bottom lip. He didn't deserve this man. "Are you being serious? Are you really going to be mine, for real?"

A bright smile lit Tobin's face. "I'm already yours, for real, but yeah. Let's do it."

The pressure in Sergio's chest screamed this couldn't be real. Surely Tobin would change his mind. Sergio didn't get to keep the people he loved. In fact, outside of Tobin, everything in his life was currently shit. He had to believe something would go wrong before Tobin actually married him. That wouldn't stop him from rushing to get this done. No way would he miss his shot. He loved Tobin, and if this happened, he would make sure Tobin always felt cherished. This would be the greatest day of Tobin's life, if it was the last thing Sergio ever did.

FOR THE MILLIONTH TIME SINCE THEY GOT home, Tobin stared down at his finger as a sense of awe washed over him. They were married. He was someone's husband. Him. Sergio had gone to huge lengths to propose to Tobin, even including their friends and family. The day had been so much more than he expected when he woke up. Tobin had only planned to have coffee with Reid today and ended up married. He couldn't get past that detail. His life just kept getting more surreal every day. If he had ever thought about Sergio wanting to marry him, which had never happened, Tobin would have expected talk of prenups and whatever else Sergio would need to do to protect himself. None of that happened. Sergio just fucking married him. Tobin was blown away by Sergio's faith in them.

Of course, after the day's excitement, Sergio had also made him go straight to bed when they got home. Tobin was too pumped to sleep, but his body felt weak. He wanted to call everyone he knew, but he also wanted to keep this to himself—like something special just for him—for at least a few days. With Sergio in the shower, Tobin needed a distraction before he exploded from too much happiness.

Tobin grabbed the remote and turned on the TV while he waited for Sergio. It was on the sports' channel as usual, because... Sergio. With a smile, Tobin almost changed the channel before Sergio appeared on the screen. It was a rerun of one of Sergio's old games. Tobin left it. He liked watching Sergio on TV. The camera kept panning between the game and the sidelines before switching to old bits of interviews and practices. Tobin realized it wasn't a rerun, but some documentary about the team. Honestly, he hated sports and never watched any of the specials that ran on any of the sports-themed channels. The TV was on mute, and Tobin did nothing to remedy that. Even though he loved Sergio, soccer still bored the shit out of him. It was a lot more interesting when Sergio played. Tobin liked watching him, but that was all Tobin cared about.

There was something about this, though. The show had Tobin's attention. What he saw mixed with something Sergio once said about not fitting in. The combination had Tobin's heartbeat thumping in his ears. As he watched, he noticed a few key details.

No one talked to Sergio. In all the clips, Sergio stood to one side while other players laughed and joked with one another just feet away. Sergio never smiled or interacted with anyone. It was... odd. Tobin felt like he just realized his child was bullied at school, or some shit. He couldn't explain how he felt. Tobin just really wanted to punch someone.

He found himself unmuting the TV, hoping to learn more. That didn't help. It was just a lone narrator, talking stats that didn't stick to Tobin's brain. Tobin ran through the faces in his mind that he had seen at the coffeehouse earlier. The only people there for Sergio had been Valor, Dawson, and Milo. Reid was married to Valor, but he was still more Tobin's friend than Sergio's. There hadn't been a single teammate or friend of Sergio's celebrating with them. Tobin didn't understand. Sergio was so, so amazing. Why didn't he have friends? Tobin was the world's biggest introvert, and there had been a surprisingly large number of people there for him. What the hell?

The bathroom door opened, and Sergio emerged, nude and drying his hair with a towel. His gaze moved toward the TV before his smiling face turned Tobin's way. "Why are you watching this?"

Tobin shrugged. "I got bored and turned on the

TV. As soon as I saw your gorgeous face, I couldn't change the channel."

Sergio tossed his towel aside and leapt onto the bed. "Bored, huh? I can't have that." He dove face first into the side of Tobin's neck and blew. A burst of laughter escaped Tobin as Sergio kissed every exposed piece of skin he could find.

"Watch live this Saturday as The Lancers' Sergio Costa is presented with this year's Player of the Year award at the Dove's Clubhouse."

"What?" Tobin accidentally screeched the question as he shoved at Sergio's chest while trying to get a better look at the TV. "Did that guy just say you're getting an award?"

Sergio sat back on his heels and turned off the TV before tossing the remote out of Tobin's reach. "Yeah. It's no big deal." He went back to kissing Tobin's neck.

"When did you plan to tell me that I need to get a tux and all that?"

Sergio didn't slow his attempts to seduce Tobin. "I didn't figure you'd want to go." His words sounded barely audible between kisses.

Tobin pushed at his chest again. "Wait. Did you plan to go without me? Are you ashamed of me?"

With a huff, Sergio finally went up onto his

elbow and met Tobin's stare. "We're married. Of course I'm not ashamed of you. I don't plan to go."

"What?" Tobin might have shrieked again, but it was too late to take it back. "You're getting what sounds like a major award, and you're not going. That's insane."

Sergio shrugged, looking unmoved. "I'm focused on us right now. You don't need to be exposed to all of those germ-infested people. It's really not a big thing."

"It's a big thing to me. I can wear a mask and I want to support you. Don't miss out on accepting a huge award because I'm sick. I'm proud of you. I want everyone to know it."

Sergio's expression didn't give any hints to his thoughts. "If I say we'll go, can I get back to making out with my husband?"

Tobin really loved being called Sergio's husband. It sounded amazing in Sergio's slight accent. Plus, the glow of happiness still hadn't worn off. "Yes."

Sergio smirked. His eyes turned seductive. "Good. We'll go figure out what we're wearing tomorrow or whatever. Right now, I have plans for you."

Love filled Tobin's chest to overflowing. Whatever Sergio's plans were, he was onboard. They had the rest of their lives together. Maybe one day he would get tired of Sergio's constant affection. He doubted it, but maybe he would. For now, though, he couldn't get enough. Tobin couldn't wait to see what each new day would bring. Everything seemed so much brighter now that Sergio belonged to him permanently. For once in his life, Tobin felt like he couldn't lose.

***

SERGIO HOPED LIKE HELL THAT HE COULD FIND A way to talk Tobin out of going to the awards ceremony. Sitting around with his asshole teammates all night was the last thing Sergio wanted to do, especially with Tobin. Right now, though, Sergio had bigger and better things to focus on—like pleasing his husband. Damn, he liked the way that word rolled off his tongue. Sergio still couldn't believe he had convinced Tobin to do a quickie marriage.

"I like this spot right here."

Tobin squirmed as Sergio licked the place on Tobin's neck he referenced. That was why Sergio liked it. It made Tobin writhe. "I hadn't noticed."

Sergio punished Tobin for being a smartass by

sucking on Tobin's hotspot. Tobin's short fingernails scored Sergio's skin.

"Tease."

A smile stretched Sergio's lips at Tobin's breathless tone. "Do something about it." Sergio couldn't stop the taunt. He loved the way Tobin's eyes flashed with determination whenever Sergio dared him to do anything.

"If you insist." Tobin pushed at Sergio's chest until he had Sergio on his back. Sergio's heart sped as Tobin bit a path down his body. His dick felt heavy, waiting for Tobin to touch it. Tobin touched him everywhere but on Sergio's cock. He shoved Sergio's thighs apart and settled between them, only to suck the inside of Sergio's groin. It was Sergio's turn to squirm. That was his ticklish spot, and Tobin knew it.

"Okay. Okay. You win. I'm a tease."

At Sergio's admission, he felt more than heard Tobin chuckle against his skin. His dick hardened even more at the sensation. Sergio's eyes fell closed. He savored the way it felt to have Tobin's lips on his body. Without warning, Tobin pushed one finger inside Sergio's asshole. Sergio's hips left the bed. A drop of pre-cum leaked out.

"Do you like that?" Tobin worked a second finger

inside as he spoke. "What would you do if I fucked you?"

Holy hell. He loved it when Tobin got turned on and lost every hint of reserve. "You know where the lube and condoms are. Why don't you find out?"

Tobin stared up the line of Sergio's body and held Sergio's gaze. "We're married now."

Sergio couldn't tell if the truth just hit Tobin or if he was simply pointing out the obvious, then realization struck. They were married now. Condoms were a thing of the past. Neither of them would ever be with anyone else again. A heartbeat passed while that new reality sank in, and then Sergio sprang into action. He could have Tobin with no barrier. Truthfully, he always could have. Neither of them had ever slipped in the past, but Sergio had never been one to take risks. In fact, before Tobin, Sergio had never even sucked anyone's dick without a condom between them. Tobin was his first in a lot of ways. Sergio couldn't wait to get inside him.

Sergio flipped Tobin onto his back and covered Tobin's mouth with his. Their tongues stroked like they were starved for each other. Sergio's dick twitched, as if trying to remind Sergio of his need. He pulled away and dove for the bedside table.

"I'm sorry. I need to be inside you."

"Why are you apologizing?"

Sergio didn't slow as he silently thanked every god that they slept nude. He didn't have the patience for undressing right now. Sergio shrugged at Tobin's question and worked on lubing Tobin's hole. "You deserve all the foreplay and I'm probably about to hurt you."

An evil-sounding chuckle slipped from Tobin's lips. His expression matched the wickedness of his laugh. "You can try."

"Goddamn." The breathless curse was all the words Sergio possessed. He couldn't explain how deeply Tobin aroused him and always kept him running home for more. Sergio dove between Tobin's thighs and shoved his way inside. He gasped at the heat of Tobin's body. His mind was beyond being a mess. All he could do was pound his dick inside Tobin over and over, trying to find his sanity. Tobin held on to the headboard and took everything Sergio dished out. The sound of harsh breathing and slapping skin surrounded them. They held each other's stare while reaching for the same goal.

A strange sensation washed over Sergio as he connected with Tobin on a higher level. His pace slowed. Sergio found himself changing angles, making love to Tobin rather than fucking him. He kissed Tobin, soft and sweet. This was his husband. The backs of Sergio's eyes burned. They were married. For however long or short their lives might be, they would spend it together. This was his family now. They were something special and beautiful. Sergio buried his face against Tobin's skin. He felt dangerously close to tears even as sweat coated his skin and he came closer to orgasm.

"I love you."

The breathless words caressed Sergio's ears as Tobin's cum filled the space between their bodies. Tobin's body gently sucked Sergio's cock, milking an orgasm from him. Sergio rode out the waves while holding Tobin as tightly as he could. He never wanted to let go. His body's pleasure had nothing on what Tobin did to his mind. For the first time in years, Sergio felt whole—like Tobin had completed him in a way he hadn't known he needed. Sergio was home. In that moment, a decision was made that he had been hovering over for almost a year. He knew what to do to reclaim his life and complete his happiness. Sergio was done with soccer.

SEVEN

ONE AMAZING THING about living in Los Angeles was that they didn't have to go far to attend Sergio's award ceremony. The private event was held at a huge and exclusive country club Tobin hadn't known existed. The biggest reason Tobin was glad they weren't far from home was because of Sergio. The moment they had walked in the door, Sergio turned brooding and quiet. His teammates were forced to introduce themselves to Tobin while Tobin fought the urge to kick Sergio in the shins. Thirty minutes in, Tobin knew they would not be staying long. Mostly because Sergio kept reminding him that they would be leaving soon.

One of Sergio's teammates appeared at Tobin's

side with a wine glass full of cold water. "I brought you a drink, since Sergio hasn't bothered."

"Thank you."

As Tobin reached for the glass, Sergio turned an icy stare Alejandro's way. "I didn't get him anything because I didn't want him taking off his mask around anyone here. I don't want him catching anything." Sergio emphasized the last words, leaving no doubt he meant the words as an insult.

Tobin's gaze swung between Alejandro and Sergio.

Alejandro smirked, but his dark gaze moved back Tobin's way, dismissing Sergio. "If you'd like to move to that empty table near the wall, I'm sure there would enough distance between everyone for you to be comfortable without your mask."

Even though Tobin was almost positive Sergio rolled his eyes, he looked away too fast for Tobin to see. Tobin eyed the nearby table. It was a large round table draped in a white tablecloth. The chairs were far enough apart that Alejandro's plan seemed airtight to him. "Sounds good."

As a group, they headed for the empty table.

Alejandro pulled out a chair and motioned for Tobin to sit. "Take this chair. That way you can see everything, but no one is sitting near you."

Tobin tried smiling with his eyes so Alejandro would know he appreciated the effort. "Thank you."

Sergio moved his chair to sit closer to Tobin. They reached for each other beneath the table. Tobin peeled off his mask. It felt good to have fresh air on his face. The room was unbelievably stuffy. Most people kept their distance while Alejandro made repeated attempts at small talk. Sergio stayed stubbornly quiet while toying with Tobin's fingers beneath the table. Tobin's nerves were stretched to their limit. Sergio was nothing like himself. There were no teasing smiles or laughing glances. Occasionally, he would kiss Tobin's temple, but then he would return to avoiding everyone's gaze.

Tobin leaned Sergio's way and kept his voice down for Sergio's ears alone. "Are you okay?"

Sergio barely glanced his way. "Yep. Are you? We can go if you're tired."

"I'm fine." Tobin forced out a chuckle. "You haven't even gotten your award yet."

"It's my job to look out for you. I don't give a fuck about an award."

Tobin bit back a sigh. He really had no clue what was going on with Sergio, but he didn't like it. Worry churned in Tobin's gut, wearing him down faster than he liked. Truthfully, he was tired and ready to go, but he also wanted to watch Sergio have his moment in the limelight.

"What do you for a living, Tobin?"

A sigh of relief nearly choked Tobin. He was unbelievably happy to have anything to focus on beyond Sergio's brooding. He focused on Alejandro. "I'm a pastry chef. Mostly I make specialty croissants for a few shops throughout L.A. Well, I did. Hopefully, one day soon, I'll be back to it. Right now, I'm focusing on my health."

"Sounds like Sergio is a lucky bastard. I love to eat. We should exchange info. My sister owns a restaurant downtown. Hooking you two up might be a great partnership. Whenever you're ready to start working again, of course."

"That would be awesome."

Tobin swore he felt Sergio's temper snap. "We should go."

In a desperate attempt at keeping Sergio calm, Tobin rubbed Sergio's arm. "It's okay. I'm feeling surprisingly good tonight. Plus, I want to watch you accept your award."

"This is the third time he's won it, so I imagine being player of the year is nothing special to Sergio."

Tobin ignored Alejandro's unhelpful interjection.

Sergio never acknowledged Alejandro in any way. "I really think we should get you home."

"Seriously, Sergio. I'm fine. You don't have to be so overprotective. I want to stay."

"Yeah, Sergio. Let your man have a little fun."

Tobin really wished Alejandro would be quiet. Sergio had something going on. Tobin needed to get to the bottom of things.

Sergio lowered his voice, forcing Tobin to lean closer to hear him. "I've spent a lot of time and money on getting you feeling this well. I'm not letting you undo all my hard work just so you can flirt with my teammates."

For a moment, Tobin's brain shut down. He didn't want to accept that Sergio had not only thrown it in his face that he had helped Tobin physically and financially but had also accused Tobin of flirting. The stress of the night and the strain of dealing with Sergio's weird mood coupled with Sergio's cruelty finally snapped Tobin. "I need to find the restroom." Tobin stood and walked away. He kept a tight hold to his phone and mask so no one would see the way his hands shook. Rage pumped through his veins. There had been a thousand reasons he hadn't wanted Sergio to help as much as he had. Yet he hadn't once expected Sergio to use everything he had done for Tobin to strike out at him. Had he been flirting? Tobin didn't think he had, but he wanted to be completely honest with himself before hiring an Uber to come get him. He had been friendly and tried not to embarrass Sergio, but he had no interest in Sergio's teammates. Tobin hadn't been flirting. Hell, he had barely spoken to anyone. He hired the car. Tobin didn't know where he was going, but he didn't want to stay. Sergio wasn't being himself, and—honestly—Tobin didn't like where things were headed. They had just gotten married. In that moment, Tobin felt like he had married a stranger. He felt a little sick. If Tobin was being honest with himself, he had caught flashes of this version of Sergio before. Tobin felt justified in his panic. He had seen what happened when people possessed two distinctly different sides before. Tobin needed to get away and think. In fact, he was on the edge of hyperventilating.

Tobin slipped outside and hid in the shadows until the car arrived. He tried not to think as he headed back to his old apartment. If he started musing over things before he was alone, he might start crying. His phone buzzed and Tobin turned it off without looking. The more distance he put between them, the angrier and more confused Tobin became. He was so, so stupid. Of course Sergio would end up resenting Tobin. Why wouldn't he? Since they met, Sergio had been taking care of Tobin. What had Tobin given him in return? Nothing. He had been so busy trying to survive that he hadn't considered he should get out of the way so Sergio could live. Fuck. He had married Sergio. Tobin hadn't wanted to be a burden to his parents. He didn't understand why he would let himself become such an albatross around Sergio's neck.

By the time Tobin reached his apartment, he was barely holding his shit together. There was a pressure in his chest. Tobin's limbs felt heavy as he climbed the stairs. As he reached the top, he realized he didn't have his keys. Everything he owned beyond his phone and wallet was at Sergio's place. He stood on the tips of his toes and tried to feel around the door frame. Being short sucked almost always. He wasn't tall enough for this bullshit. Tobin tried hopping up and down to quickly feel around each inch of the doorframe. The door opened and a guy wearing nothing except workout shorts stared out at Tobin.

"What are you doing out here?"

Tobin blinked. He recognized Lucky as one of Damon's regulars, but they had never spoken. "What are you doing in my apartment?" He tried not to drop his gaze and eye Lucky's body. Lucky did some modeling and looked the part. He had abs that definitely drew the eye. It was hard, but Tobin kept his gaze locked on Lucky's stare.

"You moved out."

Fuck. Tobin's shoulders fell. Damon had given his apartment away. If he had been thinking, he should have realized that was a possibility. It seemed he really had been too wrapped up in himself lately. He hadn't realized he was making Sergio resent him or that Damon would need a tenant. Damon couldn't go forever without the rent.

"Sorry to have bothered you." Tobin turned away.

Lucky stepped out. "Wait. Would you like to come in for a few minutes?"

Tobin cast a longing look toward the open door behind Lucky. This had been his home for nearly six years. He had started his business here. Tobin had completely abandoned his life for Sergio. It looked like he would have to start over with nothing now.

"No, thank you. Like I said, I'm sorry I bothered you."

"You'd be doing me a favor," Lucky said, keeping

Tobin from running away. "I can't figure out your stove."

Tobin tried not to show how beat down he felt. "It's your stove now, but yeah, it's tricky." He let Lucky lead him inside.

Lucky spoke over his shoulder as he headed for the kitchen. "I imagine, if you're ready to move back, that it's still your kitchen. Damon just offered this place to me as a place to crash for a while. I'm definitely not his first choice to live here. In fact, he made it pretty clear this is your place."

Walking away from Sergio turned out to be the final straw for Tobin. It seemed life had officially broken him, because Tobin gave no fucks about himself at the moment. "No. I thought to crash here tonight, but it's no big deal." Tobin's voice gave out on the last word and he had to clear his throat. Lucky eyed him a little too closely for Tobin's comfort while he explained how to use the complicated professional oven that he had bought with his first month's salary. The shock was slowly wearing off and the truth was setting in. Tobin knew he would fall apart soon. He didn't want any witnesses when it happened.

"Rich guys suck."

Tobin blinked at Lucky's seemingly from

nowhere statement. Then he caught sight of the clock. He realized he had been standing there, saying nothing and staring at nothing for several minutes. "I'm sorry. I guess I zoned out."

"Stop apologizing."

Lucky braced his palms on the countertop behind him and pushed, using his perfect muscles to easily lift himself up onto the counter—like he wasn't mostly undressed. Tobin tried hard not to stare at Lucky's body.

"The rich ones are always disappointing. They always think they've bought you. The moment you don't fall in line." Lucky slashed his hand across his throat. "Cut you down to size, so you don't forget your place."

Tobin wanted to say that wasn't his story, but he wasn't so sure that was true. He did feel like Sergio had been reminding him of his place. After all, that was why Tobin left.

"I feel really, really stupid." Tobin didn't know where the confession came from, but the words simply slipped from his lips. A tear slid down Tobin's cheek. He quickly swiped it away. He refused to fall apart. "I should let you get back to whatever you were doing."

Lucky slipped from his spot on the counter and

padded over to the sink. He grabbed a few paper towels and wet them. As Tobin looked on, Lucky swiped the paper towel over his eyes, removing makeup Tobin never would have guessed was there. That wasn't what held Tobin frozen in place. As the makeup disappeared, the bruises it kept hidden appeared.

Lucky tossed the paper towels in the trash. "You're not stupid. You should stay. At least until you figure out where you're going for the night."

Tobin's eyes fell closed. His heart sank and reality set in. Life was so much harder for everyone than it needed to be, and Tobin was an idiot for thinking for a single second that he was in the same category as Lucky. Sergio needed him for reasons he hadn't yet articulated, but he had definitely deserved better from Tobin than Tobin had shown tonight. He had to fix it.

AIR WOULDN'T INFLATE HIS LUNGS LIKE IT should. Sergio worried his heart might stop if he didn't find Tobin soon. After searching the country club high and low, texting Tobin nonstop, and having a complete meltdown, Sergio headed home. Tobin wasn't there. The instant those dumbass words had left his lips earlier, he had regretted them. Tobin's expression. Goddamn. He had looked devastated—like Sergio had punched him in the face. Sergio admitted he may as well have. He knew Tobin carried a lot of guilt over Sergio taking care of him the last six months. Tobin talked nonstop about getting back to work and paying Sergio back. That was ridiculous, of course. Not only had Sergio felt no financial burden whatsoever, Tobin was his heart and husband. It was Sergio's job to take care of him. There was no excuse for using that to lash out when he had lost his patience.

Sergio wanted to make Tobin understand, if he could. Anything he said wouldn't excuse what he had done, but Sergio had to try. First, Sergio had to find Tobin. He had never been more terrified in his life, and that was saying a lot.

After searching the house, Sergio tried to decide where to go next. He didn't think Tobin would go to his parents'. If he hadn't leaned on them through cancer, he wouldn't go to them because of Sergio. Reid was out because he was married to Valor. If Tobin ran to anyone, it would be Damon, which was really a relationship dynamic Sergio didn't understand. Unlike Sergio, Tobin had parents. Tobin didn't need a substitute parent. Yet Tobin never shut Damon out the way he did everyone else. It was odd because Reid was Tobin's best friend. If anyone should be Tobin's protector after what Sergio had done, it should be Reid. But no, Tobin would go to Damon. Sergio felt that in his gut. He opened the back door to head back out. Tobin stood on the other side.

The air left Sergio's lungs. Tobin looked a mess. His eyes were bloodshot, and his face was pale. Sergio didn't hesitate. His heart needed Tobin to be okay. He swept Tobin into his arms and kicked the door closed. Tobin silently let it happen. He clung to Sergio's neck as Sergio headed for their bedroom. They never should have gone to the awards tonight. Not only had Sergio known it was a bad idea, Tobin wasn't up to this much drama.

At the edge of the bed, Sergio set Tobin on the mattress and started undressing him. He worked in silence. It didn't matter why Tobin had decided to come home. Tobin's health came first. To that end, Tobin deserved an apology and an explanation. So Sergio just picked a place and started talking while he pulled off Tobin's shoes.

"Before we started dating, I was with this guy Lee for about a year. I wasn't in love with him or anything, but I thought he was pretty fucking perfect. He had me thinking I might like to settle down. Then, not long before I met you, I found out he was sleeping with half the guys on my team." Sergio's chest hurt. He hated this, but he kept talking. Tobin deserved better from him. "I know you weren't flirting with Alejandro, and I never should've said that. Alejandro is still dating Lee, which I don't care about, but he was trying to rile me with you. I just..." Sergio's shoulders fell as he worked on unbuttoning Tobin's shirt. "I can't lose you. You always have my back and I guess I didn't feel like you did tonight. That's not your fault. I get that I don't talk to you about work, but also no one wants to hear about anyone's exes. It was just the idea of you with anyone else, much less one of those assholes, made me lash out. You didn't deserve it. I wish I could take it back. I don't expect you to understand or forgive me. It's too late for that, I know. I just wanted to explain and apologize. You have no idea how sorry I am that I ruined us. I love you and I'm devastated that I didn't act like it when it mattered." Sergio bit his tongue to stop talking.

Down to just his pants, Tobin settled onto his side and patted the bed, inviting Sergio to join him. Sergio didn't hesitate to strip down to his pants and crawl into bed next to Tobin. Tobin snuggled into Sergio's arms with his head on Sergio's chest. He took an audible breath. The sound squeezed Sergio's heart. He wanted to kick his own ass for exhausting Tobin. Sergio truly hated himself in that moment. He wished Tobin would scream at him, but he also didn't want Tobin to waste any more energy on him. Tobin's silence was killing him.

"Do you know how I met Damon?"

Sergio's brain skipped a beat. He hadn't expected that to be Tobin's first words. It seemed an odd change in topic, but Sergio was happy to talk about anything else. "Your dad said he found you broke down on the side of the road."

He felt Tobin shake his head. "I dated his son."

Sergio kept a tight hold on Tobin. Anything Tobin wanted to talk about, they would. "I didn't know Damon had a son. Why do your parents think he found you on the side of the road?"

Tobin shrugged. "Because that's what I asked Damon to tell my parents after his son punched me in their driveway and then ripped the wiring out of my van so I couldn't leave."

Sergio fought a wave of rage. He wanted to find this guy and kill him. It didn't matter he was Damon's son and likely matched the behemoth in size. No one touched his husband. Tobin kept talking. He kept Sergio hostage with his words.

"Damon took me home, pretty determined to tell my parents everything and take whatever fallout that came from having a son he couldn't help. All I wanted was to never see either of them again. So, I begged him to lie and then never speak to me again. I'd had enough of the empty promises to change, the controlling, and the abuse. Mack dictated everything I wore, ate, and did. It took me over a year of dating him behind my parents' back to realize I wasn't Mack's boyfriend. I was his possession. By the time Damon drove me home that day, the skin I kept hidden underneath my clothes was more bruises than skin, but I was done." Tobin took an audible breath. "Nobody in the world knows any of that except Damon and me. And now you, of course."

"And Mack," Sergio said between clenched teeth. All he saw was red. He had never been more enraged.

Tobin stroked his stomach, as if trying to calm Sergio... or himself. "No. Mack committed suicide two days later." Sergio deflated. There was nowhere to go with his outrage. Before Sergio could ask any questions, Tobin steered the conversation their way, reminding Sergio why he should feel like shit. "Mack left this long note behind about how it wasn't my fault that he was fucked up, and I realized that it was nobody's fault. Mental illness is just this ugly beast that eats everything and everyone around it. Some people just don't adjust to meds and they fight everyone, including themselves. Mack just didn't want to fight anymore. At the time, I was dealing with a lot too. When I met Mack, I was in the home stretch of fighting cancer the first time around. My hair was just starting to grow back. He reminded me of those things constantly—that he had fallen in love with me when I was unlovable. It wasn't love, of course. But when you said what you said at the awards ceremony, it was like I was right back to living that life—like I was being reminded that you own me, and like you were two people. One of which I don't know at all."

"Goddamn, *bebé*. I am so sorry. I don't own you. You own me. It's not your fault that I'm—"

Tobin covered Sergio's mouth with his hand, cutting off his apology. He lifted his chin and met Sergio's stare. "This isn't about making you feel guilty. I'm simply explaining why your words took out my knees and sent me running. The point is, neither of us talk about the things that hurt us. You don't talk about work. I don't talk about why I've always been so determined to face everything alone. We're married now. I'm your husband. Tell me that your teammates are assholes and you hate them. Tell me you're miserable playing soccer."

Sergio's heart skipped a beat. Everything inside him froze. "How did you know that?"

A sad smile touched Tobin's lips. "I can see it on your face when you leave for every game and practice, and when you come home. Until tonight, I didn't really put it all together, but it all makes sense now. I think you tried to tell me after our first night together. In your own way, you've been hoping I would notice." Tobin eyes filled with tears, breaking Sergio's heart. "You can talk to me." Tobin's voice cracked and Sergio thought he might be the one who cried. "You don't have to carry everything just because I'm sick. I will get better and we will be together for seventy years. You can count on me. I shouldn't have left tonight. We're a team. As soon as you said that shit to me—in my heart—I knew you didn't mean it. I know you're a good man. We are in this life together. I will put my foot in Alejandro's ass, if you want, and I will hold your hand while you decide what you want to do. Just talk to me so I know what you need."

"I want to retire." Once the confession burst

from his lips, the rest came pouring out. "This season has been hell. I don't get along with anyone anymore, and all I can think about is coming home to where I'm wanted. At the beginning of the season, I was determined to stay because I knew everyone wanted me to quit. Now I just don't care anymore. I'm passing the age where most guys retire and everything that I have hurts. Being with you, that's all I care about. I'm done."

Tobin nodded. "Okay." A smile exploded across Tobin's face. "I can't wait to have you home all the time."

Something about Tobin calling this place home and pouring out his heart undid Sergio. He rolled and buried his face in the crook of Tobin's neck. Sergio always felt safe and at peace when he held Tobin like this. He was on the verge of falling apart. He needed to be in Tobin's arms. Tobin held him and stroked his back.

"I love you. I'm so sorry I almost ruined us by being dumb."

He could hear the smile in Tobin's voice when he spoke. "Mark my words, I'll be the dumb one, eventually. Plus, I shouldn't have left. I love you. You're everything to me."

Sergio didn't deserve Tobin. Tobin was sweet

and loving. Sergio liked to have his way and would likely always run roughshod over Tobin. Except that Tobin was so amazing that Sergio wanting his way meant he wanted Tobin to have everything Tobin's heart desired. He wanted to spoil Tobin and be present for every breath Tobin took. He was done with soccer, but he wasn't done living. They would be happy for the rest of their long lives. Sergio would make sure of it.

TOBIN STARED AT THE CEILING WHILE SERGIO'S breathing deepened. A smile kept tugging at the corners of his mouth. The night had started as complete shit, but this part was heaven. They had survived their first fight. Tobin felt pretty good about that. They might have had a moment of stupidity, but they were strong. Tobin knew they could face and survive anything together. It was odd but seeing Lucky's bruises had startled Tobin back to reality. He knew Sergio. Sergio wasn't controlling. He wasn't like Tobin's ex or whoever had hit Lucky. Sergio was good. That meant Sergio was going through something that Tobin didn't understand, and Tobin needed to be there for it—the way Sergio had been for him since day one. They had been so good together; it hadn't really occurred to Tobin to think about the baggage they had brought into this relationship. From now on, though, they would be better. This crazy night would make them stronger.

"Baby?"

"Hmm?"

Tobin smiled at Sergio's hum against his throat. "We should get ready for bed, if you're falling asleep."

"I'm not sleeping."

Tobin's smile grew at the obvious lie. After another minute passed, Sergio's body jerked, as if he had been startled awake.

"*Mi alma?*"

"I'm still here."

"We should get ready for bed before you fall asleep."

A snort escaped Tobin. "I love you. How did I end up with such a hardheaded man?"

Sergio shifted onto his elbow and touched his lips to Tobin's. It was such a sweet kiss that Tobin immediately forgot everything else. Sergio was beautiful—inside and out. He left Tobin breathless. Tobin couldn't wait to spend the rest of his life with Sergio. That sounded like the perfect future to him.

His insides trembled as Sergio stroked his stomach. It was the lightest touch, but it set Tobin's skin ablaze. He could not be more in love with this man who was like still waters.

"You looked so fucking sexy tonight in your tux," Sergio said, moving to kiss Tobin's ear. "I'm not surprised at all that everyone tried to flirt with you. Everyone kept looking your way."

"They were trying to figure out why you'd marry a bald guy." Even to Tobin's ears, he sounded breathless.

Sergio leaned away and held Tobin's stare. He looked serious again. "Is that really what you think?"

Tobin shrugged. He hated that Sergio wasn't being Tobin's laughing boy tonight, but he didn't want to lie. "I guess I don't see what you see in me right now. My hair is gone. I've lost all the weight I could possibly spare. This definitely isn't the height of attractiveness for me. I'm kind of broken down right now."

"You're still you. There's no one more beautiful. You're my soul."

Damned if Sergio didn't sound like he meant it. "And you're mine." No matter what life threw at them, that would always be true. Tobin believed that to the deepest recesses of his heart. They were meant to be.

"I'll make you see what I see," Sergio promised as he lowered his head once more.

Tobin believed. He knew Sergio was full of magic and light. Sergio could do anything, and Tobin had years and years left to watch the beauty unfold. Their forever looked more beautiful every day. Right now, Tobin wanted to focus on their kiss. This moment. Their next breath. They were strong and happy. Most of all, they couldn't be broken.

EIGHT

INSIDE THE CAVERNOUS ballroom at one of L.A.'s oldest and most expensive hotels, Damon unabashedly watched while Sergio "nom-nomed" on Tobin's cheek. Tobin shook with laughter. Reporters snapped pictures alongside family. Sergio and Tobin were completely oblivious to everything but each other. Their wedding and reception had happened around them. The couple were in a bubble of blindingly beautiful love. Everyone and everything else were nothing more than background noise and scenery to the couple who were obviously lost in each other. It was everything Damon had ever wanted for Tobin.

Tobin's hair had grown back, and he looked healthier than he had in years. Mack would have been thrilled. Damon knew Tobin couldn't look back on Mack with any fondness, but Damon also knew his son had genuinely loved Tobin. Mack had done terrible things that couldn't be excused. Damon hoped he had made up to Tobin for his son's sins. But Damon also—in a way no one would understand—got to hold on to a small piece of his son through Tobin. As long as Tobin lived, Mack did too. As long as Tobin was happy, Damon got to believe Mack was at peace. In life, Mack never had peace beyond the small bits Tobin gave to him. No one had been strong enough to save him, but Damon loved Tobin more than anyone else still breathing for trying. He understood better than anyone how much it cost Tobin.

Damon's eyes skimmed through the room, catching sight of a few more familiar faces. Lucky was getting chatted up by someone Damon had seen before but couldn't place. He didn't take the time to figure it out before looking away. Lucky was... something else. Damon hadn't quite figured him out. He was a custom body decked out in chrome and specialty paint over burned-out wiring that had also been caught in a flood. His incredible beauty and youth hid a money pit labyrinth of unfixable bullshit. Damon didn't know why he hadn't given up on the guy. Any other sane person would. Maybe it was because he couldn't live with himself if he lost another soul because he wasn't strong enough to save them. Someone had to be there for the ones who were a little broken.

A cheer and whistles rent the air, pulling Damon's eyes back the happy couple's way. After all, he was here for Tobin. Sergio had tossed Tobin over his shoulder and was headed for the door. A smile snapped to Damon's lips and a chuckle stuck in his throat. Even from across the room, Damon experienced a blast of secondhand embarrassment. Tobin had his face hidden, but even his ears were red. It seemed Sergio was done sharing Tobin for the evening. Damon was surprised they had lasted this long.

A hand landed on Damon's shoulder and squeezed. He glanced over to find Lucky staring back at him. His steel-colored eyes shone bright with laughter. As always, Damon fought the strange flutter in his gut when Lucky was around. "Are you feeling like the proud papa tonight?"

Damon fought the urge to immediately hide his heart. He knew Lucky didn't know about Mack and Tobin. No one did. Lucky was simply making a correlation between Damon's age and his care of

Tobin over the years. Still, he fought the urge to tell someone how much he wished his son could be there and be happy. He wished this had been his son's life with Tobin without all the ugliness. "Somewhat. It's good to see Tobin like this."

Lucky nodded. He kept his gaze locked on the happy couple while Damon couldn't look away from Lucky. Without looking Damon's way, Lucky kept up his end of the conversation. "I'll go with you, if you'd like."

Damon blinked at the odd statement. "Where?"

"To your son's grave."

Damon refused to show an ounce of surprise. Lucky had an odd way of always knowing everyone's secrets. It was like he saw too much. Maybe that was why the guy never dated anyone who didn't hurt him. People didn't like having their souls exposed. Damon tore his gaze away from Lucky. Tobin and Sergio were gone. It was time to go. "Nah. You're young. Go do young shit."

"You act like you're an old man."

Damon snorted. He couldn't keep his gaze from swinging back Lucky's way. "I definitely am by comparison."

Lucky's eyes swam with laughter. "All right, old man. Then you should definitely go do something with me and make sure I don't end up in trouble. You know how I can be."

Damon groaned as he draped his arm across Lucky's shoulders and steered him toward the door. "Fine. You win. Let's find something semi-adultish to do before you end up in god only knows what kind of trouble." Damon just prayed the scent of Lucky's cologne didn't land Damon in even bigger danger. Sometimes he could be pretty damn dumb like that.

———

RETIRING SO HE COULD SPEND EVERY DAY WITH Tobin was one of the best decisions Sergio had ever made. He was also glad they had decided to wait to have their big wedding until Tobin could enjoy it. Tobin hadn't stopped smiling all night. Sergio didn't want to look away. Happiness radiated from Tobin, making him glow. Sergio had always been the type who liked to play. He was a kid at heart. Carrying Tobin through the hotel and to their room—for all to see—was a blast. He loved the sound of Tobin's laughter.

By the time he dumped Tobin on the bed in their suite, Tobin's face was as red as it could get. Sergio didn't know if it was from embarrassment or all the blood rushing to his head from being over Sergio's shoulder. He didn't stop to find out before covering Tobin's body with his and claiming Tobin's mouth.

If he got any happier, Sergio would burst. It didn't matter that they had already been married for months. Today had been about celebrating them. Sergio wanted to make every day like this one for Tobin. That was the only way he could think to give Tobin a quarter of the happiness Tobin had given him since they met.

Sergio pulled away and brushed noses with Tobin. "Do you think anyone noticed we left?"

A laugh burst from Tobin, making Sergio's heart smile. "You're ridiculous."

"Meh. I prefer to think of myself as hilariously efficient. You weren't forced to say goodbye to everyone, and we can send cards later."

Tobin wrapped his arms around Sergio's neck. His light green eyes flashed with devilry. "Is that what happened? You saved me? And here I thought you couldn't wait to get me in bed."

Sergio reached between them and went to work on undoing Tobin's pants. "Nope. It was all about the not shaking hands thing. I know you're in remission, but you shouldn't be touching everyone."

Tobin's arms fell away in exaggerated mock

surrender. "Fine. I won't touch anyone. I'll just stay right here, lonely and neglected. Starved for human touch." He sniffed loudly.

Sergio shook his head at Tobin's antics. He didn't slow in divesting Tobin of his clothes. "I'll just take these uncomfortable clothes off so you can suffer—naked in your isolation."

With his gaze locked on the ceiling, Tobin sniffed again. "If you must."

With his bottom lip held between his teeth to keep from laughing, Sergio stripped Tobin bare. The moment he had every inch of Tobin's perfect skin on display, Sergio stood and stripped. Tobin's heated gaze slid Sergio's way, so Sergio went slow. He purposely teased Tobin with each newly bared inch. Tobin was hard and his cheeks were flushed. Sergio became the victim in his game. He tortured himself by moving slow. Sergio couldn't take it any longer. He needed Tobin's kiss. His heart demanded it.

Sergio crawled onto the bed and straddled Tobin's body. He held Tobin's stare as he lowered his head. Sergio swore he felt their emotional connection like it was a physical thing. As their lips met, Sergio's eyes fell closed, but he felt like he could see clearer than he ever had in his life. He saw years and years unfolding before them. Each one happier and brighter than the next. Sergio knew in his heart that they were soulmates. They had been born to be together. Not only would they always watch each other's back, they had saved each other. There was no one else out there for Sergio. They should have gotten married the day they met, since they had been fated to end up like this. He knew happily ever after didn't mean there would never be bumps in the road, but they were strong. There was no battle they couldn't win together. They were the only team Sergio needed. This was his forever home.

KEEP AN EYE OUT FOR THE NEXT CANDIED Crush, *Beautifully Unfixable*.

Please consider leaving a review at the retailer where you purchased this book. Reviews really help with a book's visibility, which allows me to continue writing more stories. Thank you, Charity.

ABOUT THE AUTHOR

Charity Parkerson is an award-winning and multi-published author with several companies. Born with no filter from her brain to her mouth, she decided to take this odd quirk and insert it in her characters.

*Eight-time Readers' Favorite Award Winner
   *2015 Passionate Plume Award Finalist
   *2013 Reviewers' Choice Award Winner
   *2012 ARRA Finalist for Favorite Paranormal Romance
   *Five-time winner of The Mistress of the Darkpath

Connect with her online:

—Sign up for my newsletter: http://bit.ly/CharityNews
   —Join my readers' group on Facebook: http://bit.ly/CharitysTribe
   —Website: charityparkerson.com

—Facebook: facebook.com/authorCharityParkerson

facebook.com/TheMenofSin

—Twitter: twitter.com/CharityParkerso

—Instagram: Instagram.com/sinnerauthor

— Bookbub: https://www.bookbub.com/authors/charity-parkerson